Ella's heart stuttered in her chest.
Is he going to kiss me again?

She answered the question herself. "I'm not going to wait to find out."

"Excuse me?" Chase said.

"Never mind." She laughed. And then, since the man stood within easy reach, she grabbed the lapels of his suit coat and hauled him closer for a kiss.

He blinked in surprise when her lips met his, but then his hands clamped onto her waist and she felt his fingers dig into her flesh through the suit's gabardine as he pulled her closer. That, as much as the low groan that emanated from the back of his throat, told her he was as turned on as she was.

Ella closed her eyes and gave herself over to the moment.

Dear Reader

I am sometimes asked if I base my characters—especially my heroines—on myself. While little pieces of my personality can undoubtedly be found in most of my heroines, in Ella Sanborn's case she is definitely a figment of my imagination. Which, I have to say, is what made her a blast to write.

Oh, to be that free-spirited and fun! I am much more conservative in both dress and personality.

And, while I am certainly not a pessimist by nature, Ella is so optimistic and resilient that I can only hope I would be the same when faced with similar circumstances.

I admire people who, rather than remaining on the mat, get up and keep fighting after life knocks them flat.

My hero, Chase, is a fighter, too. Although he and Ella, of course, approach problems very differently. He is much more analytical and serious, whereas she laughs in the face of adversity.

I hope you enjoy Ella and Chase's story as much as I enjoyed writing it. Drop me a line with your comments. You can find me on Twitter, Facebook or through my website, www.jackiebraun.com. I look forward to hearing from you.

Happy reading!

Jackie Braun

AFTER THE PARTY

BY
JACKIE BRAUN

MILLS &
BOON

Published in Great Britain 2014
by Mills & Boon, an imprint of Harlequin (UK) Limited,
Eton House, 18-24 Paradise Road, Richmond, Surrey, TW9 1SR

© 2014 Jackie Braun Fridline

ISBN: 978 0 263 91080 3

Harlequin (U__) _____ p_____ ___ p__ ____ ___ __ _____
renewable a__ _d recyclable products and made from ____ grown in
sustainable __ _____ _____. ___ _____ ___ _____ _____
to the legal ____ environmental _____ ___ ___ _____ __ _____

Printed and ___ ____ bound in Spain
by Blackpri__ ____ ___ _____

Jackie Braun is the author of more than two dozen romance novels. She is a three-time RITA® Award finalist, a four-time National Readers' Choice Awards finalist, the winner of a Rising Star Award in traditional romantic fiction and was nominated for Series Storyteller of the Year by *RT Book Reviews* in 2008. She lives in Michigan with her husband and two sons, and can be reached through her website at www.jackiebraun.com

This and other titles by Jackie Braun are available in eBook format from www.millsandboon.co.uk

For Mom. With all my love.

PROLOGUE

"I SEE A HANDSOME man in your future."

Ella Sanborn fought the urge to roll her eyes at the older woman reading her palm. Ella could be naive at times. She was too trusting for her own good, or so she had been told on more than one occasion. And she was superstitious, hence today's visit to a fortune-teller. But she wasn't a complete fool. She was pretty sure Madame Maroushka told every young, unattached woman who darkened her door the very same thing.

But finding a man wasn't what had brought Ella here. She leaned over the table and studied the lines that crisscrossed her opened hand, wishing she could make sense of them herself.

"What about a job? Do you see anything on there about a job? Preferably one with decent hours, paid holidays and medical benefits."

Madame Maroushka's scarf-wrapped head jerked up. In her heavily accented English, she asked, "You are single, no?"

"Yes."

"But you are not interested in a man?"

"I'm not." She said it resolutely, thinking of her ex-boyfriend, Bradley Farmington.

He'd been as loyal as a prostitute, dumping her right

after her father's legal troubles began. So much for true love. After the insider-trading charges leveled against Oscar were dropped, Bradley had sent her a note of apology. He felt bad about the way he'd handled things and claimed that he'd never *really* believed her father was guilty of anything. He'd been overly worried about his pending membership into an elite Manhattan social club. Ella forgave Bradley for bailing on her. She figured he'd done her a favor. He'd shown his true colors. A lot of her so-called friends had.

But Ella hadn't dated anyone seriously since.

"He is very good-looking, this one," the older woman crooned.

Ella shook her head. "I have more pressing problems than my social life right now."

"But he is rich." Madame Maroushka's wily smile revealed a gold front tooth. Hmm, Ella thought, the fortune-telling business must pay pretty well, which reminded her...

"I'd rather have a job."

"Land a wealthy husband, my dear girl, and you would not have to work ever again."

"Yeah. So I've heard," Ella replied dryly, thinking of her former stepmother's snarky advice.

Camilla Sanborn would know a thing or two about landing wealthy husbands. She'd married Ella's father at the height of his success and then left him to marry another billionaire when Oscar's fortunes changed. No, thank you, Ella thought. She would pay her own bills, starting with those that were past due, just as soon as she had a job.

She nodded toward her palm again and asked Madame Maroushka, "Are you getting any vibes about the sales position at La Chanteuse on Thirty-Third?"

She'd submitted her résumé more than a week ago and, even though the manager had said the post needed to be filled immediately, Ella had heard nothing. Working in retail wasn't where she saw herself employed indefinitely, but in the interim, she would take what she could get. Besides, one of the perks of working at the ladies apparel store was a 20 percent discount on merchandise, and there was a leather handbag that was calling Ella's name.

It was hell being a fashionista on a thrift-store budget.

"My gift does not work that way. It tells me what it tells me while I study your palm. I see a man," the woman insisted a second time. "He is tall—"

"Dark and handsome," Ella finished impatiently.

"Hey, you want me to continue or you gonna read your own palm?"

Ella blinked in surprise. Just that quickly, the woman's accent had relocated from East Europe to North Jersey.

"Uh, sorry. Go on."

"Very well." With her accent now back in the Baltic, Madame Maroushka continued. "He is lonely, this man. And not dark, at least not how you meant. I see fair hair and light eyes. He is searching for…someone."

In spite of the pressing nature of her visit, Ella couldn't help but be intrigued. "But is he single?"

Jersey made another appearance in Madame Maroushka's speech. "Whaddaya think? I just said the guy was lonely and searching."

"Yes, but the two conditions are not mutually exclusive," Ella felt the need to point out. "Last month, I went on a date with a guy who claimed to be lonely and looking for love. He also happened to be married."

A detail he'd failed to mention until his wife showed up at the restaurant where they were dining, wielding a set of knitting needles and threatening to pluck out Ella's eyes.

The corners of the palm reader's mouth turned down in consideration before she nodded. "Okay. Point taken. But this one is single." She traced a finger over one of the creases on Ella's palm again.

"So, is this handsome stranger looking to hire a woman?" Ella asked.

When Madame Maroushka's eyebrows shot up, Ella squeaked, "Not for *that!* I'm talking about a legitimate job. I can cook reasonably well, and I know how to scrub a toilet."

She'd had both a housekeeper and a cook while growing up, but she'd learned as an adult. Neither skill would put her fashion merchandising degree to any better use than the sales gig at La Chanteuse, but Ella couldn't afford to be picky.

"I do not believe he seeks either a housekeeper or a cook," the fortune-teller said with a shake of her head. "I see the two of you at a social gathering."

"Like a party?"

"I believe so. He is wearing a tailored dark suit and the two of you are drinking champagne poured from a bottle with a fancy black label."

Ooh. It must be some shindig if the host had sprung for Dom Perignon. Momentarily sidetracked, Ella scrutinized her palm.

"Am I wearing the fuchsia cocktail dress with the ruched waist that I got on sale last month?" The tag was still attached to the sleeve and she'd been debating returning it. She really couldn't afford the designer original, even if she'd gotten it for a steal. But if she had someplace to wear it— "No. Never mind." She shook her head for emphasis. "I'm not going to be attending any parties. I don't need to improve my social life. What I need is a job. Better yet, I need a career."

A sales job in retail was definitely the bottom rung of the ladder when it came to a career in the fashion world, but her well-connected ex-stepmother knew a lot of people in the industry. People whose ears she'd bent with vicious gossip and outright lies. No one wanted to hire Ella if it meant crossing Camilla. Whatever. Ella wasn't averse to working her way up as long as she was working.

Madame Maroushka frowned, causing the drawn-on mole just above her mouth to dip into one of the lines that feathered out from her lips. "This…this is most unusual."

"What?"

"I see the party *as* your career."

"What? Do you mean I'm like a party planner or something?"

"Could be," the older woman allowed.

"I like parties. I've been to enough of them." Both the fancy variety in her previous life as the daughter of a high-powered Wall Street wheeler-dealer and the casual, keg-of-beer kind since her father's fall from grace. She nibbled her lower lip, an idea hatching. "How much do you think people get paid for planning them?"

Madame Maroushka shrugged. She was back in Jersey when she said, "Beats me. It probably depends on the kind of people you plan the parties for and the kind of parties they want you to plan. Know what I mean?"

In other words, the deeper their pockets, the more they would be willing to pay. That made sense.

"I know a lot of people with deep pockets," Ella murmured half to herself. Until her father filed bankruptcy, she'd even called some of them her friends.

Madame Maroushka glanced at her watch, her tone brisk and all business when she said, "Time's up. Thanks for coming. Here." She handed Ella a coupon.

"What's this for?"

"The printing place two blocks up on the opposite side of the street. My nephew owns it. He is handsome and single," she said with a smile. When Ella just stared at her, Madame Maroushka said flatly, "He's running a special on business cards. You get five hundred for the price of four with this coupon. If you want to be a party planner, you'll need cards and lots of them."

Why not? Ella thought. What did she have to lose? She paid Madame Maroushka and headed to the print shop where she blew the last of her meager savings on business cards and promotional fliers, which she then spent the following two days distributing all over Manhattan.

Two weeks later, her efforts appeared to have paid off. She had a meeting with a client, and a very deep-pocketed one, too. There was only one downside to the job and it was a doozy. The party she was being asked to plan was a wake.

CHAPTER ONE

CHASE TRUMBULL'S MOOD was in the toilet when he strode through the main doors of the New York skyscraper that housed Trumbull Toys' corporate offices. It was a gloriously sunny Friday in June, just four hours shy of quitting time for those who punched a clock, with the weekend weather forecast calling for clear skies and highs in the eighties. But it felt like a cold and cloudy Monday given the rumors that were circulating and the grim financial news he'd just received.

Even so, he wasn't blind, much less dead. So, in spite of his foul mood, his steps slowed and his gaze detoured south to take in the view.

As backsides went, the one on the woman who'd stopped midstride in front of him was one of the finest he'd seen in a long time. It was firm, nicely curved and packaged in a narrow zebra-print skirt that clung to its contours like a glove to the proverbial hand. The legs that extended from the skirt's meager hemline were the perfect complement to a first-class ass. And the shoes—black with red soles that ended in daggerlike four-inch heels… Well, it was all he could do to hold back his groan. And that was before she bent over to retrieve something from the lobby floor.

Of course, this was neither the time nor the place to indulge base instincts, even if a toned butt, killer legs, animal-print miniskirt and stilettos ticked all of the boxes on his libido's wish list. He concentrated on the company's projected second-quarter profits. Those certainly were dismal enough to banish the triple-X fantasy that had started to play in his mind like the featured film at a bachelor party.

As it was, the sizable slump in sales from the previous four quarters had the board of directors on edge and stockholders beginning to defect. The finger was being pointed in a direction Chase didn't want to look. And then there were those damned rumors.

The woman straightened, turned slightly and, catching sight of him, smiled apologetically, leaving asymmetrical divots in her cheeks. One dent was midway between her mouth and ear. The other, just to the side of her lips.

"I'm sorry. I hope I wasn't in your way."

"Not at all," he lied politely. Another oddity in her features registered and good manners deserted him. He blurted out, "Only one of your eyes is blue."

"The other is brown. It makes it a little tricky when I have to fill out any official forms."

"I'm sure." He realized he was staring, and asked, "Did you lose something just now?"

"Actually, I found something." She smiled again and held out her hand. A single copper coin decorated its palm.

"That's a penny."

"A *lucky* penny," she corrected. "It's an omen." When he frowned, she said, "You know, a sign. A good one in this case. I'm here about a job."

The first layer of fantasy peeled away. Chase was too practical to put stock in omens. As for luck, he was of the firm belief that people made their own. His uncle was a case in point. Elliot Trumbull was the founder and creative genius behind a multibillion-dollar business that he'd launched four decades earlier with toys that remained beloved and collected the world over. Vision, passion, hard work—those were the ingredients for success. Not luck, even if Chase could admit that Elliot had run into a spate of the bad variety lately.

"And you think finding a penny on the floor in this lobby is going to help you with that?"

The woman shrugged. "It can't hurt. Right?"

Well, she had him there.

Together, they started for the bank of elevators, where nearly a dozen people outfitted in conservative business attire waited. They greeted Chase with nods and murmured "Good afternoon," before parting like the Red Sea. When the doors of the first elevator slid open, not one of them boarded it.

Chase was used to this. When Elliot had brought Chase back to New York from the company's California office eighteen months earlier, he'd come with the express purpose of turning around Trumbull Toys' flagging bottom line. Unlike his uncle, who was officially at the helm and remained the creative force, or Owen, Elliot's son, who was known to flirt outrageously with female workers, Chase believed in running a tight ship. As a result, employees feared him. When possible, they went out of their way to avoid him. The young woman, however, stepped inside the elevator without a moment's hesitation. Then she caught the doors before they could close.

"Isn't anyone else coming?"

She directed the question to the crowd at large. Several of them flushed. A few of them stammered incoherently. An intern from the marketing department looked as if he might faint.

"They'll catch the next car," Chase replied on their behalf.

"Oh. Okay." She released the doors and they shut.

Chase punched the buttons for floors two and seventeen. Human Resources was located on two. Top management offices, including his, were on seventeen. When the bell dinged and the doors opened one floor up, however, the woman made no attempt to leave.

"This is two," he prompted. "Aren't you getting off here?"

She blinked at him, one brown eye and one blue clouded with confusion. "No. I thought you were."

"Why would *I* be getting off here?"

"Well, you're the one who pressed the button," she reminded him.

"The human resources department is on this floor." He pointed down the corridor. "It's the third office on the left. That's where all job applicants check in to fill out paperwork before being sent on to department heads for their interviews."

"There must be some mistake."

"It's all right." He held the doors to keep them from closing. "You probably just misunderstood."

"No, what I mean is, I'm not here for an interview. I've already got the job. I'm meeting with my client on the seventeenth floor."

That was when it hit him. No…no…no.

Chase realized he'd muttered his objection aloud when she said, "Excuse me?"

He released the doors and they closed, sealing him inside the elevator with a woman who was every man's fantasy and, now that he knew her identity, Chase's worst nightmare.

Tone grim, he said, "You're the party planner."

"Guilty as charged. I'm Ella Sanborn." She sobered slightly. "Don't tell me *you're* Mr. Trumbull. Er, I mean you sounded…different on the phone."

He could only imagine.

"One of three. I'm Chase. You're here to see Elliot. He's my uncle."

"I am so sorry to hear he's dying."

Jaw clenched, he replied, "My uncle is not dying."

Her brow wrinkled. "But when he called, he said he wanted me to plan a wake. An Irish one. For him."

Chase rubbed the back of his neck just above his shoulders where a tight knot was already starting to form. "My uncle isn't Irish, either."

"I don't understand."

"A common occurrence," Chase remarked.

His uncle's quirkiness left a lot of people scratching their heads. Lately, he also had become unpredictable and absentminded to the point that some members of the board of directors were questioning his mental fitness and ability to continue as the head of the publicly traded company. Rumor had it that they were close to having the votes to do it. Chase didn't want to think what the board members who were still on the fence were going to think if his uncle went through with this wake.

Too late Chase realized that Ella thought his comment was directed at her.

"I can be a little naive at times, but I'm not an idiot."

"I didn't mean to—"

"Oh, my God. It's all a joke, isn't it?"

Chase frowned. In the span of a few seconds he'd gone from being contrite to being confused. "What?"

"The job, the supposed interview. Somehow Bernadette found out about my new business venture, and she put you up to this."

The elevator stopped on the fifteenth floor. Three men from the product development department were waiting to board. With one glance from Chase they scuttled away like crabs at low tide.

When the elevator was under way again, he asked, "Who is Bernadette?"

"She's my stepsister. Ex-stepsister, actually. Her mom

and my dad are divorced now." Ella paused to add a dramatic, "Thank God!" Then, "But that hasn't stopped her from trying to make my life miserable."

"Well, this is no joke. My uncle is serious about wanting an Irish wake."

"Even though he's not Irish and he's not dying."

"He has his reasons." Ones Chase didn't quite understand and couldn't agree with. "My uncle can be… He's often…" At a loss for how to describe the man who had raised him from the age of ten on, Chase finished awkwardly, "He's just like that."

Especially lately.

"Like what?" Ella asked.

Chase clamped his lips closed. He didn't want to believe the rumors circulating about his uncle's deteriorating mental capacity. He certainly wouldn't help spread them.

Greeted with his silence, Ella said, "That's okay. I'd rather meet him and make up my own mind anyway."

Unfortunately, Chase had a pretty good idea of the opinion Ella Sanborn would form once she did.

The elevator dinged, heralding their arrival on the much vaunted seventeenth floor of the Trumbull Toys empire. Several years ago, Ella had seen a television special on Elliot Trumbull and his place of business. It had made toy stores seem drab and restrained by comparison. But when the doors opened, the sight that greeted her left her not only disappointed but baffled.

"Is something wrong?" Chase said.

"This is the fabled Trumbull Toy Company?" she asked before she could think better of it.

Chase frowned. "What were you expecting?"

Well, she hadn't been expecting beige walls and a nondescript sitting area. Where was the life-size Randy the

Robot that she'd seen in the TV special? And the basketball hoops? The foosball table and minitrampoline?

She laughed weakly. "I guess I was expecting toys."

"Those are gone. I found they were too distracting and sent the wrong message to employees. This is a place of business."

Yes, and that business was toys. But she decided not to press the point.

Two women and a man sat at a horseshoe-shaped reception desk talking into headsets as they tapped away on keyboards. All three were dressed as conservatively as Chase in the muted colors Ella associated with storm clouds. Admittedly, she liked bright hues and fun prints, hence her zebra skirt and the poppy-red blouse. Still…

As a unit, they glanced in Chase's direction, but just like the group in the lobby, and the men who'd tried to board the elevator several floors later, not one of them maintained eye contact for very long. Ella's gaze slid to Chase. She could see why. In his dark suit, perfectly knotted tie and polished wingtips, Chase Trumbull cut an imposing figure. She shouldn't have found him approachable much less attractive. But she did. Oh, yeah, she did, all right.

She blamed the attraction she felt on his cowlick. She was a sucker for cowlicks, and his was a beaut. That little whirl of sandy hair just to the left of his part simply refused to go along with the rest of his fastidiously styled locks. It reminded Ella a bit of herself. She wasn't one to go along with the crowd, either.

All sorts of superstitions were attached to cowlicks. Some people saw them as the mark of the devil. Others insisted they were a sign of good luck. Ella's best friend, Sandra Chesterfield, meanwhile, claimed that men with cowlicks were exceptional lovers. She'd read an article to that effect on the internet. If that was true, a man with one displayed so prominently at his hairline must be…

Ella fanned herself.

"Hot?" Chase asked.

Yes, and that made two of them. But she smiled and said, "I'm fine. Cool as a cucumber."

His brows furrowed momentarily. Then, to the woman seated on the left of the reception desk, he said, "This is Ella Sanborn. She's here to see Elliot."

"Yes. He's expecting her."

"My uncle's office is the third door on the left."

The door in question was closed. Ella asked, "Should I knock?"

"Just once and then go right in. If you wait for him to answer, you might wind up standing there all day."

It seemed rude to barge in, even if she was expected. "You're sure he's not busy?"

Chase consulted his watch. "Oh, he's busy. It's nearly race time."

"What?"

"You'll see." One side of his mouth rose. It wasn't quite a smile, but it was the closest she'd seen him come so far. It softened his features and left her a bit dazzled. It also made her wonder what Chase Trumbull would look like with a full-out grin plastered on his face and amusement lighting his eyes.

"Good luck. Of course you don't need it," he said solemnly. At her puzzled expression, he added, "You found that penny in the lobby."

"I did." Ella replied with an equal amount of seriousness, even though she was pretty sure that he was teasing her.

He disappeared into the first office, whose door bore a brass plate etched with Chase Danforth Trumball III, Chief Financial Officer.

She sucked in a breath and proceeded to the third door, passing one with a brass plate marked Owen Scott Trumbull, Chief Operating Officer. The nameplate on the third door wasn't brass. It was bright red, and its white carnival-esque script read, Elliot Trumbull, Purveyor of All Things Fun. In spite of her nerves, she found herself grinning. After she knocked and the door opened, that grin changed into delighted laughter.

Now this was more like it.

It wasn't an office. It was every young boy's fantasy, complete with a race track that snaked under, over and around the spacious room's eclectic furnishings.

"You're just in time," said a man teetering on the top rung of a ladder that overlooked the track.

Even though he was older now, she recognized him from the television program. Elliot Trumbull in the flesh. And he was indeed the purveyor of all things fun.

No stuffy business attire for him. He was dressed in a professional racecar driver's jumpsuit, complete with half a dozen endorsement patches sewn on the sleeves and chest. In one hand, he held a flag; in the other, a bright orange starter pistol. As Ella stood transfixed, he fired the gun into the air—the bullet a blank, she assumed, since it didn't take out any ceiling tiles—and declared the race under way. On the track, three vehicles about the size of her palm whirred into action.

"They're sound activated by the pistol," he told her. "After that, a computer takes over and ultimately decides the race. Care to place a bet on the winning car?"

"Ten bucks on number seventy-seven," she replied, without stopping to wonder if she had enough money in her purse to cover her wager.

"Why that one?" he wanted to know.

"Because blue's my favorite color and seven is my lucky number."

"Sound reasons to pick it then," he agreed without a trace of his nephew's mockery in his tone. "I always go with red for the same reason. You must be Ella."

After climbing down from the ladder, Elliot picked his way over the track to her. She placed his age at late sixties and his weight at one-eighty with most of it centered at his waist. He had a shaggy mustache and a mop of salt-and-pepper hair that gave him a decidedly Einstein vibe.

"I'm pleased to meet you, Mr. Trumbull."

She would have shaken his hand, but he took the one she extended and kissed the back of it instead. Make that Einstein meets Sir Galahad.

"Call me Elliot. We don't stand on formality around here." His bushy brows pulled together in a frown and he muttered, "At least I don't. I run a toy company, for the time being, at least. That should be fun, don't you think?"

"I do," she agreed.

"Good. At least someone does. Would you like something to drink?" Instead of offering the usual coffee or tea, he said, "My secretary makes the best strawberry malts this side of the Mississippi. Probably the best on either side, come to think of it."

Ella's mouth watered at the offer, but she shook her head. "No, thanks."

"All right. Then, have a seat and we'll get started."

The room didn't have a proper sitting area. Instead, it boasted two white chairs that resembled hollowed-out eggs on clear plastic stands, and a cushioned porch swing that hung from the ceiling on a pair of thick chains. It creaked when Ella sat down and set it into motion.

"Comfortable?"

"Very. My grandmother has a swing like this at her house in New Jersey."

Elliot beamed. "My grandmother had one, too. I loved that swing. Did some of my best thinking on it as a boy. That's why I have one here. What do you think of my office?"

She glanced around and couldn't hold back her smile. "It's a lot fun."

"Exactly. Let me ask you something, Ella. Do you think toys are only for children?"

She shook her head. "Aren't we all children at heart?"

"Not all of us," Elliot said. Then, "Ah, speak of the devil."

She glanced over to find Chase looming in the doorway. His expression was one hundred and eighty degrees the opposite of his uncle's inviting grin. He looked positively grim.

"Sorry to interrupt. I just wanted to remind you that before this afternoon's meeting with the board of directors we need to go over some reports."

"Meetings and reports," Elliot muttered before hooking his thumb in Chase's direction and adding in a not-so-confidential whisper, "All work and no play, that one. I guess some good genes skip a generation."

She bit back a smile. It was impossible not to find the older man charming, even if his humor came at his nephew's expense.

Chase remained stoic. "It's important. When do you think you'll be finished here?"

"Oh, it will be a while yet." Instead of pointing out that they had barely gotten beyond introductions, Elliot said, "The cars are only on their third lap." Then he whistled softly. "Look at your blue car, Ella. It's pulled ahead of the silver, but my red one is still in the lead."

"Come see me when you're done in here." Chase nodded politely in her direction.

When he turned to leave, however, Elliot said, "I'd like you to stay, Chase. I value your opinion."

"You already know how I feel about the party, Uncle."

"Wake, you mean."

"You're not dying."

"Oh, but I am. Professionally speaking anyway." To Ella, he said matter-of-factly, "My board of directors thinks I've lost my marbles. That's ironic, don't you think, given that I make toys for a living?"

"I...I..." At a loss for words, she glanced at Chase.

His cheeks were flushed a deep shade of red. "No one is saying that," he ground out.

"To my face," Elliot conceded. "But we both know what is being said behind my back."

"When I find out who started the rumors we'll sue them for slander," Chase declared.

"I will be out of a job by then. Owen is only too happy to take my place. He's my son," Elliot informed Ella. "He has the head for this business, but not the heart. That apparently skipped a generation, too."

"Ah." She nodded, not knowing what else to do.

To Chase, Elliot said, "The writing is on the wall. Don't think I don't know it. I may be slowing down, becoming a little forgetful, but I'm not stupid."

The older man sounded weary, resigned.

In contrast, Chase's tone was infused with urgency. "That's why we need to talk, put together a plan of action before this afternoon's meeting."

"All right," Elliot conceded with a sigh. "But after I speak with Ella. Stay, Chase. Please."

Chase was too tall to sit comfortably in either of the egg-shaped chairs, so he joined Ella on the swing. His feet remained firmly planted on the floor, bringing the swing to a halt. It was time to get down to business.

Calm. Collected. Confident. She chanted the three words in her head as she exhaled slowly and pulled a small notepad from her purse. She'd jotted down several questions she figured a party planner would ask.

In her most professional voice, she said, "Let's start with the basics. When do you want to have your wake?"

"Memorial Day would have been fitting, but it's passed."

He sighed. "What about the weekend before the Fourth of July? We could have fireworks at night."

Ella might not have planned any parties, but three weeks to prepare seemed doable. Until she asked, "How many guests will there be?"

"Six, maybe seven hundred."

Her mouth went slack. A party for sixty would have left her panicked. How on earth was she going to pull off a party for six or seven *hundred?* And in less than a month?

"Uncle Elliot, be reasonable."

"I am being reasonable. If I'm going out, I'm going out with a bang. What do you say, Ella?"

"Well, the, um, timeline is a little tight for a gathering of that size."

"You're right."

She relaxed until Elliot said, "Let's push it to August. My Isabella died in August. August twenty-seventh." His expression dimmed. In a bewildered voice, he asked, "Can it really be three years?"

"I'm sorry," Ella told him.

"I couldn't have started my company without her. She was my rock."

The race cars whizzed past on the span of track that wound under Elliot's desk. Just that quickly, his attention was diverted. He clapped his hands together, eyes once again bright, and crowed, "My red car is still in the lead! Have your ten dollars handy, Ella. There are only three laps left." Afterward, he scratched his head. "Now, where were we?"

"The guest list," she prompted, still feeling dazed.

"Right. Definitely seven hundred. In addition to friends and family, I have a lot of acquaintances in business and the community at large who will want to pay their respects." He snorted before adding, "And my competitors will want to come and dance on my grave. The media, too."

"Media?" Chase asked, sounding alarmed.

"That's right. I plan to invite reporters from several news sources, both tabloid and mainstream. You can't keep those vultures out anyway. I might as well open the doors and the bar to them. That way, they won't be circling in helicopters overhead."

"Isn't that the truth?" she replied, thinking of her father's treatment by some so-called journalists. She glanced up to find Chase studying her. Clearing her throat, she asked Elliot, "Do you have a location in mind, then?"

"My house. Estate, I guess is more accurate. It's in the Hamptons. We could set up tents. The grounds are quite expansive." He chuckled. "I just happened to think, the name of my estate is The Big Top. What about Three Ring Circus for the theme?"

"I thought the theme was Irish wake," Chase and Ella said at the same time.

"Right, right." Elliot nodded. "What if it's both? What do you think, Ella?"

She nibbled her lower lip to give herself a moment to think. A circus-themed wake for a man who wasn't dying? For the first time since seeing Elliot's call, she wondered if perhaps Madame Maroushka had gotten her palm confused with someone else's.

"Well?" Elliot prodded.

"While there is nothing wrong with a party that has two distinct themes, marrying them can become, um, tricky. That's especially true when they are so, um, so…different," she finished, hoping to sound authoritative even if she was making things up as she went along.

"But it can be done?" Elliot asked hopefully.

Uh-oh.

"It can be. But it would take a lot of planning. Months, say, to do it right. Are you willing to wait that long?"

"No." He sighed.

Ella nearly did, too.

"I suppose that answers that question," Chase said. He looked as relieved as Ella felt. Then he asked, "May I make a suggestion, Uncle?"

"By all means."

"If you are determined to have a party, why don't you go with the circus theme and save the wake idea for another time?"

Elliot scratched his head. "I don't know. I really want to have a wake. Ella?"

She'd already done some research on wakes. Besides, she had a clown phobia, and was pretty sure any big top-type bash the size Elliot wanted would have to include at least a few of the painted-faced performers.

"The circus theme is overdone."

"What?" Chase asked at the same time Elliot said, "I should have known."

"An Irish wake will be very, um, cutting edge."

Chase gaped at her as if she'd grown a second head. "Really?"

"Really. This is the first one I've ever planned," she added truthfully.

"She should know, Chase," Elliot said. "She's the expert."

Ella worked up a smile that she hoped didn't reveal her newbie-ness.

"Look, Uncle Elliot, you claimed you want my opinion, so I'm offering it. Throwing a party right now—"

"A wake," Elliot corrected.

"That only makes it a bigger mistake. Calling it that will feed the rumor mill."

Elliot shook his head, his expression patient, but still resigned. "I appreciate your input, my boy. Really, I do. But if I am going to be turned out of the company I started, I will do it on my own terms."

"But a wake?"

Elliot looked every year of his age when he replied, "It's fitting. What is forced retirement but another form of death for someone like me?"

The whir of the race cars broke the stretch of silence that followed. Elliot's sober expression brightened when the little vehicles shot into view.

"Ella! Look! Your fortunes have changed. I think you're going to win the race!"

He hurried over to the ladder, arriving at the top step just in time to wave the checkered flag. As he'd predicted, the blue car marked with number seventy-seven was the first to cross the finish line.

"Congratulations, young lady!" To Chase, he said, "Pay her for me, will you, my boy? Our wager was for ten dollars."

Chase stood to retrieve his wallet from the rear pocket of his pants. He pulled two fives from his billfold and handed them to her. Afterward, he didn't return to his seat. He paced to the window, where he stood, arms crossed, back to the room, a quiet yet imposing presence whose mood she could not quite gauge. He wasn't angry. That much she could tell. Frustrated? Perhaps. But something else was going on.

She did her best to ignore him for the next twenty-five minutes as she culled as much information as she could from Elliot. The task wasn't easy. The man was full of suggestions for his wake, but he kept going off on tangents. One moment, he was talking about beverages and the next he was relating a story about a fly-fishing excursion in the Rockies, the only common thread between the two being grape soda.

As they wrapped up, they made plans to meet again the following week, by which time Ella promised to have a mock invitation ready for Elliot's approval, and some menu suggestions.

What did one serve at an Irish wake? Surely the fact that Elliot was so offbeat gave her license to be creative.

"You haven't discussed the budget," Chase said, turning back from the window. They were the first words he'd uttered in nearly half an hour.

"Ella can spend whatever she needs to spend. Money is no object," Elliot replied on a shrug.

A muscle ticked in Chase's jaw and he shoved a hand through his hair. Every strand fell back into place, except for those caught up in the cowlick. They staged a rebellion and remained erect. Sandra's claim about men and cowlicks had Ella sucking in a breath.

Chase's gaze met hers. She swore the air crackled with electricity, almost as if he could read her mind.

"Well?" he challenged.

Her mind went blank except for X-rated thoughts. "Wh-what?"

"How much do you think you'll spend?"

Money. Right. She would have been relieved, except that she had no clue as to the cost.

"I promise to show restraint," she replied with what she hoped was a reassuring smile.

He looked far from reassured. "And what about your fee? What do you charge for your services?"

Her fee? In truth, Ella hadn't thought that far ahead. "I, um, I charge a percentage."

"Of what?"

"Of the overall cost," she told him without stopping to wonder if that sounded reasonable.

"What about a contract? Did you bring one with you?"

"Good heavens, Chase. Stop badgering the young woman." To Ella, Elliot said, "It's the lawyer in him, I'm afraid. In addition to his business degree, he has a law degree, too."

That made him handsome, imposing and apparently too educated for a sense of adventure.

"He has a point," she told Elliot. "We probably should have something in writing."

"Why? Did you know I sold my first toy to a store on Thirty-Fourth with a mere handshake?"

"Randy the Robot," Ella supplied with a smile.

Not surprisingly, Chase was frowning. "That was more than four decades ago. We live in different times, Uncle."

"Which is too damned bad, if you ask me," Elliot replied. "I'm a good judge of character. I trust Ella."

"Thank you for that, Elliot," she began. "I appreciate your vote of confidence, really, but—"

"Oh, all right," the older man broke in. "If it will make you both feel better, I'll put it in writing."

Chase relaxed visibly at the news. That was until Elliot reached behind him on the desk, tore off a square from the boxed calendar set and scribbled something on its back. He handed the paper to Ella.

It read: *I, Elliot Trumbull, being of sound mind and body, promise to pay the delightful Ella Sanborn whatever the heck she decides to charge me for one Irish wake.*

His signature was scrawled below it.

It was all she could do not to burst out laughing.

"May I see that?" Chase asked.

She gave him the paper and wasn't surprised when he let out a soft curse.

After she and Elliot wrapped up their meeting, Chase accompanied her to the elevator.

"I guess you were right," he said as he pushed the down button.

"About what?"

"That penny you found in the lobby. It really was lucky."

She might have smiled had he not added, "See that you don't abuse my uncle's trust."

Incensed and offended, she muttered the first thing that came to mind. "What a waste of a good cowlick."

"Excuse me?"

"Never mind."

When the elevator doors closed a moment later, however, she had the satisfaction of seeing Chase try to pat down his hair.

CHAPTER TWO

CHASE HEADED FOR the decanter of aged scotch the moment he arrived home. It was after eight o'clock and he had yet to eat dinner, but that didn't stop him from pouring two fingers and then downing them in a single gulp.

The fiery liquid scorched his throat, but did little to chase away the bitter taste in his mouth.

Damn the five members of the board of directors who were being so spineless!

Damn the investors for their lack of faith!

Damn his cousin for being so disloyal!

And damn his uncle for…for…

Chase set the glass on the counter and ran the back of his hand across his mouth.

None of this was his uncle's fault—even if Elliot seemed to have thrown in the towel.

A wake, dammit. One to which the media would be invited. To Chase's dismay, what he found himself focusing on was the very attractive woman hired to plan it.

He ran a finger idly around the rim of his empty glass as he recalled Ella Sanborn's intriguing face, pinup curves and mile-long legs. When his mind threatened to slip into fantasy mode, he forced himself back to the present. Ella was sexy and gorgeous and quirky enough to keep a man guessing what she would say next. But was she competent to handle such a huge job?

She'd fallen into the gravy, he thought, recalling the "contract" Elliot had signed. It was dealings such as this that put the more conservative members of Trumbull's board of directors on edge. Handshakes and hastily scrawled "contracts" were not how Fortune 500 companies were supposed to do business.

His phone rang as he contemplated pouring himself a second drink. A glance at the caller ID had him considering letting it go to voice mail, but there was no sense prolonging the inevitable.

"What do you want, Owen?" he said in lieu of a greeting.

"Chase. We're cousins. We grew up the under the same roof. Do I really need a reason to call you?"

They might have grown up together, but they had never been close.

"You only remember that we're related when you want something," Chase replied. "So what is it?"

He heard an exaggerated sigh and then, "I'd hoped to speak to you in person after the board meeting."

"That wasn't a meeting. It was a frigging blood-letting. How could you do that to your own father?" Chase's temper flared anew just thinking about it and his tone turned sharp. "You all but hung him out to dry."

"No. I was honest with the board when I was asked my opinion of his mental state. When are you going to admit that my dad needs to retire? If he goes now, he goes out on a high note and the company can be saved."

"For God's sake. It's his company!" More than that, Trumbull Toys was Elliot's life. Chase expected Owen, of all people, to understand that.

"It *was* his company. Now it belongs to the shareholders." Owen took delight in adding, "You were the one who convinced him to take Trumbull Toys public."

A move that had made good sense six years earlier, but one Chase regretted now.

"Then they need to be made to see reason."

"What they're seeing are the most recent sales projections. My father…has lost his edge."

"He hasn't lost anything."

"We both know that's not true," Owen replied with a hint of sadness in his tone. "He lives in his own little world half the time."

"It's called being a creative genius. It's what makes him so good at coming up with new toys."

"And so lousy at being a father," Owen shot back.

"Is *that* what this is about? Family grievances?"

"I wish!"

"Do you?"

"Look, his memory, his judgment, both have gotten worse since my mother died. When are you going to admit that, Chase? You may not think so, but I'm looking out for the future of Trumbull Toys. Dad needs to step down."

"He needs…he needs a little help."

"On that much we agree. Meanwhile, he's not up to leading the company."

"He built it from nothing. Without his vision and creativity, there would be no company. How can you side with the stockholders and those board members who believe he should be ousted?"

Chase hated to consider it, but he couldn't help wondering if Owen might be responsible for the dementia rumors that were only succeeding in making a bad situation worse.

"It's not personal. It's business. And it's a fact, Chase, that Trumbull Toys is no longer setting market trends. We're following them."

"I tell you, there's a leak. Someone inside the company is selling us out to our competitors before our new toys are officially launched."

It was one of the reasons Chase had tightened up the

loose, anything-goes atmosphere that his uncle had allowed to flourish. Chase knew he was viewed as a tyrant as a result. Even his uncle complained that the new policies went too far and took all of the fun out of the office. But Chase wasn't sure what else to do. He owed it to Elliot to try everything possible to protect the legacy the older man had built.

"There's no friggin' leak!" Owen countered, his tone surprisingly adamant.

"How do you explain the fact that Kellerman's managed to come out with its remote-controlled dinosaurs just two weeks before we did?" Chase replied.

Kellerman's was their biggest rival in the industry. At one time, its founder, Roy Kellerman, not only had worked at Trumbull, he'd been one of Elliot's closest friends. They'd parted ways decades earlier after a falling-out that, from what Chase gathered, had been more personal than professional, as it involved his Aunt Isabella. Her funeral marked the first time the two men had spoken since becoming business rivals. Elliot claimed they'd buried the hatchet. If that were true, Chase was pretty sure it had been buried in Elliot's back, because not long after that Trumbull's business woes had begun.

Owen replied, "They did their research. They knew that's what boys in the five- to ten-year-old demographic wanted."

"They stole our idea!" Chase insisted.

Two remote-controlled dinosaurs, one named Chomp-a-saurus Rex and the other called Chomp-action T. rex, was more than a coincidence or savvy market research.

"There's no evidence of that. Look, Chase, I love my father, too, but he hasn't been the same since Mom died. He's slipping. This wake nonsense is just one more example. He's no longer fit to lead."

Chase ignored the weariness in his cousin's tone. It was easy to do since Owen seemed so damned eager to slide into the top spot, despite the fact that Elliot had made it plain he wanted Chase to be his successor.

Even with Elliot out of the way, Owen would need the board's backing to take the helm. More and more, it appeared he had it.

Elliot's wake could very well be the final nail in his professional coffin. In Chase's mind, it didn't bode well that it was being planned by a woman who believed in lucky pennies.

The following Tuesday, Ella splurged on a taxi to get to her appointment with Elliot. Since she was taking a cab rather than hoofing around Manhattan, she decided to wear her favorite pair of high heels. They were black patent leather with silver detailing on the vamp. They added four inches to her height. Unfortunately, if she wore them for too long, they also left her hobbling. But, damn, they looked great paired with the hot pink skinny jeans and printed peplum top that she'd gotten for a steal at a sample sale in the Garment District.

The door to Chase's office was closed and the man in question was nowhere to be seen when Ella arrived on the seventeenth floor. She told herself she was relieved, since he made her so nervous. But she called herself a liar when the door to the office next to his opened and he stepped out. Her pulse took off like the miniature race cars in Elliot's office.

He turned then, and she blinked in confusion at the stranger who stared back at her. The man was the same height and build as Chase. His coloring was similar, too. But his features were sharper, his nose slightly longer. No cowlick mocked his tidy hair.

"Well, hello." Piercing blue eyes lit with interest when he smiled.

"Hi. You must be Owen Trumbull."

"That's right. And you must be Ella Sanborn."

His smile was friendly, if flirtatious. He shook her hand, holding it a little longer than was necessary. Owen certainly had none of his cousin's reserve.

"Yes."

"My father tells me you're going to throw quite a party for him."

"Yes. I'm here to go over some of the plans."

Owen smiled again. "Mind if I sit in?"

"That's up to Elliot."

Chase's presence the other day had made Ella nervous, since it was clear he didn't approve of the wake and, for that matter, didn't trust Ella not to take advantage of Elliot. Still, she found herself glancing toward his door.

"He's out," Owen told her. "Won't be back for a while."

Just as well, she thought, refusing to be disappointed.

The racetrack was quiet when she and Owen entered Elliot's office. The older man was seated behind his desk rather than on top of it, and a sheaf of papers was scattered over the blotter. He was clad in appropriate, if boring, work attire. Conservative suit. Starched white shirt. His only bow to fun was the tiny hot air balloons that speckled his bowtie.

His eyes lit up when he spied her and a smile wreathed his face, pulling his jowls firm. "Ella! If you aren't a sight for sore eyes."

"Hello, Elliot. I hope I'm not disturbing you. We did say nine o'clock?"

"We did." With that he pushed the papers into a pile to one side and propped his reading glasses on top of his head. "I'm eager to see what you've come up with."

"And I'm eager to hear what you think."

She pulled a folder from the oversize handbag that was

doing double duty as a briefcase, and passed it to him. Rather than opening it, however, Elliot transferred his gaze to his son.

"Is there something you wanted, Owen?"

"Not particularly."

"Then you may go."

The request was made with a surprising amount of authority from a man who otherwise came across as easygoing.

"What? I can't stick around? Offer my advice on your little party?"

Nothing about the gathering Elliot had in mind could be classified as little. But what Ella found interesting, perhaps even telling, was that Elliot didn't correct his son and use the word wake, even though he had been quite explicit on that point with Chase.

"You don't care about this party, Owen."

"Neither does Chase, but when you met with Ella last week, he was here. You told me so yourself."

Although Owen's tone was matter-of-fact, his reply struck Ella as petulant, childish. Some form of sticky family dynamic was at work here. Exactly what it was, she wasn't sure. But if the drama of her stepmother and stepsister had taught Ella anything, it was that she didn't want to be in the middle of it.

"Maybe I should come back," she murmured.

Elliot apparently didn't hear her. His gaze still on Owen, he said, "Chase might not approve of the party, but at least he cares."

"Right. Saint Chase. For a moment I forgot who I was talking about." Owen made a mocking bow in her direction. "It was nice to meet you, Ella."

The door closed behind him with a thud. Elliot stared at it, frowning. When he glanced back at Ella, he seemed perplexed.

"Why are you here again?"

"Your party," she said slowly.

Elliot continued to frown. About the time she became uncomfortable, he grinned and his expression turned impish.

"Wake, you mean. Let's call it what it is."

Muffled laughter, both masculine and feminine, greeted Chase when he stepped off the elevator.

The sounds emanated from his uncle's office. Elliot's laugh brought a smile to Chase's lips. No one—whether child or adult—was proof against the man's booming guffaw. The feminine laugh, however, had a different effect on Chase since he had a pretty good idea to whom it belonged.

Ella Sanborn.

She'd been on his mind a lot the past few days. She'd starred in one very explicit dream over the weekend, although that wasn't the reason he'd nearly called her. He needed to speak to her about a matter that had nothing to do with thigh-high black silk stockings and a lace-edged push-up bra.

With the board's official vote looming, the party his uncle had her planning had the potential to blow up in all of their faces. In the meantime, Ella was privy to some information that Chase would prefer she didn't share with anyone…especially the media.

As he approached his uncle's door, it opened and both occupants stepped out.

"I can't wait to see the changes to the invitation," his uncle said before turning to his secretary. "Marlene, did you finish that guest list I asked you to compile?"

"Yes." The ever-efficient secretary pulled out a large envelope and handed it to him. "Here is a hard copy, and I've already sent the file to Ms. Sanborn's email address."

"Excellent. Thank you. Reward yourself with some chocolate drops."

Candy-coated chocolate drops were a staple at the Trumbull Toys headquarters, and Elliot was liberal in doling them out for jobs well done. Marlene, however, remained sober-faced. Chase knew his presence, rather than any concerns over her diet, was the reason. He was a wet blanket, his appearance in a room all that was necessary to dampen the occupants' enjoyment.

His gaze skimmed Ella then. She looked fresh, lovely… fun. Not exactly professional in those sexy high heels, but definitely approachable. She turned then and caught sight of him. Her smile was reserved but nonetheless lethal, and caused a knot to form in his stomach.

"Hello, Chase."

When his tongue threatened to tie into a knot similar to the one in his gut, he frowned.

"Is something wrong?" she asked.

"No."

"Excuse me a moment," Elliot said to Ella. "Apparently my signature is needed on some papers. I told Marlene she could forge it, but she's a stickler for rules."

Thank God, Chase thought, and his frown deepened.

"Do you ever smile?"

Ella's question caught him off guard. "What?"

"I just realized that in the short time I've known you, I haven't seen you smile. Not once."

"And you find that odd?"

"Well, yes. I do find that odd. I doubt an hour goes by that I don't smile or bust out laughing."

"Because laughter is the best medicine?"

Mismatched eyes narrowed. "You're mocking me, but yes. Laughter is the best medicine, and it beats the alternative, which is crying."

"So, I should be grinning like a loon and laughing all the time lest I start bawling like a baby?"

"No, but you work at a toy company. You should be... happy!"

"Wow. Now you've determined that I'm unhappy. Are you always so quick with your judgments?"

"No." She frowned. "At least, I try not to be."

"But you've made an exception in my case."

"Ooh. I've stepped in it good, haven't I?"

"Yes." He waited for her apology.

But Ella said with maddening directness, "Am I wrong? Are you happy?"

Who asked such bold questions? Certainly no one else in his uncle's employ.

"Some of us take our responsibilities seriously. We have to," he added, thinking of his uncle's flighty temperament and just how much was at stake. That brought Chase back to his concerns. Some unscrupulous journalists would pay Ella handsomely for insider tidbits about Elliot. God help them if one already had. "Which reminds me, I'd like to have a word with you in private."

"Right now?"

"If you and my uncle are finished, yes."

"Ella and I are done," Elliot replied, coming around the reception desk. "But I thought that you and I had plans." He scratched his head. "Or did I get that wrong? Don't tell me I wore this damned monkey suit and canceled my morning walk in the park for nothing." He smiled at Ella. "I walk rain or shine. It's good for circulation. Owen bought me a treadmill for Christmas so I wouldn't have to leave the building to go for a walk, but you can't feed the pigeons on a treadmill."

"You're right, Uncle. We do have plans." Chase had scheduled a brunch meeting with Sumner Thurgood, one of the few board members who at least seemed hesitant to throw Elliot under the bus. He turned to Ella. "I guess our talk will have to wait."

"I'll look forward to it." Her wry smile made it clear that she was lying.

Momentarily lost in those teasing, mismatched eyes, he replied honestly, "So will I."

CHAPTER THREE

CHASE TOLD HIMSELF he was merely checking one more thing off his long to-do list when he arrived at Ella's apartment building later that same day.

He'd found her Lower Manhattan address with no problem, but he hesitated before getting out of his car, feeling uncharacteristically nervous. Maybe dropping in on her without advance notice wasn't such a good idea. Not only was the hour late for a social call, he wasn't expected and she might not be alone.

Might? Who was he kidding? A woman who looked like she did wouldn't hurt for male companionship, even if it was closing in on ten o'clock on a weeknight.

These were sound reasons to head home and call her in the morning to schedule a proper meeting. Instead, he disregarded both common sense and good manners and got out of his car.

Her building didn't have a doorman. Overall, security was sorely lacking. The main entrance was propped open with a brick, making its antiquated buzzer system obsolete. He removed the brick after entering and made a mental note to mention it to Ella. In the small foyer, he found her name on the bank of mailboxes. Apartment 4C. He glanced around for an elevator, but saw only stairs. It explained a lot about her toned derriere, he decided, as he started up to the fourth floor.

She answered on the third knock. Two things clued him in that she hadn't used the peephole before flinging open the door: The shock that registered on her face when she saw him and what she was wearing. The cotton boxer shorts ended high on her thighs and the tank top fit snug enough across her breasts to make it obvious she wasn't wearing a bra. He willed his gaze to remain on her face as he opened his mouth to speak. He needn't have bothered. She slammed the door shut in his face.

That made two of them who were surprised.

He was turning to leave when he heard the knob jiggle and the hinges squeak. Ella stood framed in the doorway wearing a neon green hoodie, cropped black yoga pants and a sheepish smile. Even dressed for a cardio workout, she was still way too sexy for his peace of mind.

"Sorry about that, Mr. Trumbull. I wasn't expecting you."

"So I gathered. Call me Chase," he said, even though the courtesy title had helped create a little distance, and he could use as much of that as possible at the moment. "You should use the peephole next time."

"I know, but I thought you were my neighbor. Her fridge is on the blink, so she's been keeping some things in mine."

The explanation made him feel marginally better, but only because the neighbor in question was female. So, he felt the need to point out, "When I came in just now, the entry door was propped open with a brick."

"Yes, I know. The guy one floor down does that for his friends. He has a band and plays his music so loud that he can't hear the buzzer."

"Have you reported him to the building's super? Anyone could walk in." And this was the sort of neighborhood where the anyones would be less than desirable.

She smiled. "You sound just like my dad."

Chase frowned. His advice might seem paternal, but it bothered more than he cared to admit that she was comparing him to her father. He cleared his throat, deciding it was time to get to the reason for his visit.

"I'm sorry to bother you at home and so late, but I needed to speak to you and it couldn't wait."

"Is something wrong?"

Before Chase could continue, a man and a woman, clothes disheveled and locked in an intimate embrace, stumbled out of the apartment next to Ella's.

"You really need to go," the woman said breathlessly, even as she made no move to release her visitor.

"I need to stay."

"My boyfriend will be back soon."

"Then let's go back inside and finish what we started," he replied suggestively.

"No."

Immediately following her refusal, they locked lips again. Moaning ensued. When the woman began to wrap her legs around the man's waist, Chase figured he knew what would come next. He turned to Ella.

"Would it be all right if we had this conversation in your apartment?"

"That's probably a good idea," she agreed hastily, backing up to allow him inside.

One step over the threshold and Chase realized that in addition to standing in her foyer, he was also in her living room, kitchen, dining room and boudoir. The one-room apartment was that small. Hell, the walk-in closet off his master bedroom was more spacious. And filled with fewer clothes, he decided after taking a glance around. All manner of apparel hung from hooks. It decorated the walls in place of artwork and spilled from the most unlikely places, including the cubbies in a small writing desk and the metal hoops of a wine rack. He was no expert on female attire, but the garments appeared designer quality and therefore expensive. Ella's eye color wasn't the only contradiction.

"This is…cozy," he amended at the last minute. If he stretched out his arms, he was pretty sure he could touch the walls on either side of the room.

She chuckled, the sound a mix between embarrassment and wry humor. "It's the size of a matchbox and a little messy right now." As she spoke, she used her foot to push something small and lacy behind a stack of fashion magazines on the floor. "Believe it or not, this is larger than my last place."

"You must have slept standing up."

"If I were any taller that might have been necessary," she agreed. "As it was I couldn't fit a bed in it. I had to make due with a foam mattress on the floor."

"Sounds uncomfortable."

Which was how Chase felt now that he was picturing her laying on that subpar mattress wearing…

He coughed. To reel in his libido, he focused on what Ella's home said about her. Real estate was expensive in Manhattan, but between the size of her studio apartment and its location, he was left to wonder how well her party planning business was doing if this place, an improvement over her last, no less, was all she could afford. Of course, maybe she spent the bulk of her income on her designer wardrobe.

She was saying, "Oh, it wasn't that bad. You'd have had a hard time of it, though. You're what, six-four?"

"Six-two," he corrected.

"Hmm. You look taller. Probably because I'm not wearing heels at the moment."

They both glanced down at her bare feet, where the sight of candy pink toenails had a disturbing effect on his pulse. He'd never thought himself a foot man. Until now.

They claimed his full attention until she rose on tiptoe and motioned between her forehead and his with her flattened hand, taking his measure. Mismatched eyes regarded him for a moment, making him wonder if he'd passed muster. Then, a few loud thuds, followed by the sound of more urgent moaning came from the hallway. Ella dropped back onto her heels and moved away.

"It's a little warm in here," she said.

Instead of taking off the hoodie, she dialed up the knob on the air conditioning unit that obscured most of the view from the apartment's lone window. The fan kicked on, blowing stale-smelling air into the room and drowning out the sounds coming from the couple going at it in the hall.

"I was just having a glass of wine. Would you like me to pour you one?"

He should say no, but after the day Chase had had, the offer was too good to pass up, even if he didn't intend to stay long.

"If it's not too much trouble."

"None at all. Have a seat."

Her request posed a bit of a problem. Unless he wanted to move the stack of folded clothes that were piled on the chair by the desk, the only other surface available was the futon, which was also Ella's bed. Even with the hum of the air conditioner, he could still hear thumps, grunts and moans coming from the hall. It was unseemly. It was disturbing. Add in a barefoot Ella, with her hoodie no match for either his memory or his imagination, and Chase felt ready to combust. So, he decided to avoid the bed and remain standing while she went to the kitchen for the wine.

Calling it a kitchen was a bit of a stretch. It was half a dozen steps away and the only things that defined it as such were the minifridge and a hot plate that sat on a dinky span of countertop next to an equally dinky sink. She rose on tiptoe and opened the cupboard over the sink. Sharing space next to the stemware were several pairs of pumps.

"You keep shoes in the cupboard."

"It's not ideal," she admitted on a laugh that again sounded more wry than embarrassed. "But I've had to get rather creative since storage space is so limited."

Shoes in the cupboard definitely rated as creative. But Chase found himself wondering once more about her business savvy. Shoes in the cupboard didn't bode well on that score.

So he asked, "Do you have an office? I only saw this address listed on your card."

She unscrewed the cap on a bottle of merlot. As she poured them both a glass, she replied, "No. I work from home."

Chase glanced at the clothes-draped desk and chair. He doubted she got much done there. A laptop was open on the floor, but that appeared to be it for technology. A cursory glance around revealed no scanner or copier or printer. A business such as hers took coordination, organization and lots of contacts. Where did she meet with those contacts? Where did she meet with her clients? Certainly not here.

She handed him the wine and he took a sip. It tasted pretty much how he had expected a vintage that came in a bottle with a screw-on cap to taste.

As if reading his mind, she said, "Sorry. It's not exactly Chateau Lafite." He was trying to figure out how she knew about the pricey French label when she asked, "Aren't you going to sit down?"

Ella pushed pillows and a fuzzy pink blanket to one side and settled on the futon, pulling her feet up beneath her. The spot open next to her looked entirely too inviting.

"No, thanks. I've been sitting all day," he told her, and then found a clear spot on the wall against which he could lean one shoulder.

"So, what did you want to talk about?"

For a moment Chase had nearly forgotten the urgent nature of his visit. "It's my uncle."

A pair of beguiling, if dissimilar, eyes brightened as she smiled. "Elliot is delightful."

"He is that." It was the other adjectives being applied that caused Chase to worry. "When we were in his office last Friday, some of what was said…well, it wasn't for public consumption."

"The part about him being forced into retirement, you mean."

So, she had picked up on it.

Chase nodded. "I brought a confidentiality agreement I would like you to sign."

The lawyer in him knew that it held little weight since he was having her sign it after the fact, but it was the best he could do.

He pulled the folded document from the breast pocket of his suit coat and handed it to her.

"I hope you can appreciate the need for discretion. If the media were to get wind of such talk…" He took another sip of wine. It tasted just as bad as it had the first time, but it wasn't responsible for the sour taste in his mouth.

"I understand."

"Besides, nothing has been decided."

"Elliot seems to think it has."

"It's the rumors." Chase stared into his wine as she studied the confidentiality agreement. For no reason he could fathom, he heard himself admit, "He's been acting more erratic lately and getting a little forgetful."

He swirled the wine in his glass, wishing for something that not only tasted better but was a hell of a lot stronger.

"And you're worried it's dementia."

"Dementia! No! God, no!" He couldn't bear to think it.

"It could be something simple, you know. Like a vitamin deficiency."

"Yeah?"

"My grandmother got a little spacey at one point. Her B-12 levels were out of whack. A few shots later, she was back to being her old self again."

Chase liked the sound of that, even if getting his uncle to see a doctor would be near impossible. It had been decades since Elliot last saw a physician. He'd refused to go for even an annual checkup since Chase's father, Elliot's twin brother, had died of a rare blood disorder. He said he didn't want to know if he, too, had the hereditary condition. Chase and Owen had both been checked, and, thankfully, were unaffected.

"In the meantime, we still have a problem. The board, or rather, several of its members have raised concerns about his fitness to continue leading the company."

"I would imagine the recent slump in sales isn't helping."

At that, Chase's gaze snapped to hers. Suspicion coiled like a snake about to strike. "What do you know about Trumbull's sales?"

"It's a publicly traded company. For a while, shares held steady even when profits began to decline, but now they are slipping, with some investors anxious about the release of this quarter's figures."

"You follow the stock market?"

She answered his question with one of her own. "Does that surprise you?"

"N-no."

The sputtered denial had barely made it past his lips when Ella started to laugh.

"It's all right. I know I don't look like the average broker, and I'm hardly an expert on Wall Street."

She was right on the first count. "But you obviously pay attention."

"My dad was…interested in stocks. Besides, when Elliot called to ask if I would plan his wake, I did a little digging online so I would be prepared when I met him."

"Ah." It made sense. Still, Chase got the impression she had been about to say something else.

"An internet search turned up a story on Trumbull stocks."

"Just one?" he asked dryly.

"Several, actually. This economy has hit a lot of businesses hard."

She was being polite, Chase knew, since the articles she'd read probably mentioned how well Trumbull's competitors were doing in comparison.

A familiar sense of frustration settled over him. "My uncle started his company after none of the big toymakers would even meet with him about his idea."

"Randy the Robot."

Chase nodded. Everyone had heard of the famous toy. A couple of generations earlier, practically every kid in the country had owned one.

"Elliot always has had an eye for what appeals to children. No one believed in him when he started out. The banks wouldn't even give him a loan. He poured his blood, sweat and life savings into developing a prototype, finding a manufacturer and personally visiting stores, begging them to put it on their shelves. And now—" He broke off, surprised to have told her all of that. He was here to make sure what she already knew didn't go any farther. Not supply her with additional information. "I'm sorry. I'm sure you don't want to hear this."

"Don't apologize. I understand. He's family and you love him. Naturally, you're angry on his behalf. It hurts to watch someone we care about suffer."

From her tone it was clear she was speaking from personal experience, which made it easier for Chase to be blunt. "My uncle is making a mistake with this party."

"Wake, you mean."

"Exactly my point." Chase rubbed his forehead. "The message he's sending to the board, to the shareholders and to his competitors is that he's giving up without a fight."

"And you think it will give credence to the rumors about his…erratic behavior and forgetfulness," she finished diplomatically.

"It certainly won't help."

"From what I read, your uncle has a reputation for being eccentric. People have come to expect that."

"But an Irish wake…" He sipped more wine. God, the stuff really was nasty.

"Are you asking me *not* to take him on as a client?"

As much as he wanted to tell her yes, Chase shook his head. "No. That decision is my uncle's."

"I'm glad you see it that way. Besides, he seems adamant about going ahead with it. If I don't plan his wake, someone else will."

Since she'd presented Chase with the opening, he took it. "About that. Can I ask you a question?"

"Sure."

"After speaking to my uncle the other day, you must know this is a large undertaking."

She blew out a breath. "Huge."

"Yes. And since his guests will include business rivals and members of the media, well, it's imperative this go off as smoothly as possible."

"I agree."

"Then you will understand that I must ask, what are your credentials?"

"My credentials."

"In the elevator the other day, you mentioned something about your business being a new endeavor. You aren't the only one to do an internet search. After the meeting in my uncle's office, I did one of event planning services in the city. I couldn't find anything on yours."

Uh-oh.

Ella swallowed and it was all she could do to keep a smile plastered on her face.

"I'm relatively new at this," she admitted.

"Yes, so I gathered. Can you tell me a little bit about your background?"

"Well, I have a bachelor's degree from New York University," she began. She should have stopped there. He appeared suitably impressed until she added, "In fashion merchandising."

"Fashion?"

"Merchandising," she added. "It's the business side of fashion."

"And now you plan parties for a living."

He scratched his cheek, looking as if he were having a hard time connecting the dots. She thought it best not to mention the role Madame Maroushka had played in this particular career move.

"How many parties have you planned?"

"The actual number?"

Chase nodded.

"Hmm. Let's see…" She tapped a finger to her lips, wondering if she should include the surprise party she'd helped throw for her friend Sandra when they were seventeen. That would make…one. Where Ella had attended scores of major galas, balls and bashes over the years, she'd never been in on the actual planning.

"Feel free to ballpark it," he told her when the silence stretched.

She decided to come clean. It was easier to do since they'd already established that keeping her on the job was his uncle's call.

"Here's the thing. I haven't actually *planned* any big parties. Yet."

Chase had been lounging against her wall, and looking pretty damned good there, too. Even better than the collection of designer scarves that hung just to his left. Upon hearing her answer, he levered away from the chipped plaster so abruptly that wine sloshed over the rim of his glass and splattered on the white area rug under his feet.

He muttered an oath, whether because of the stain or her lack of party-planning experience she couldn't be sure.

"Sorry," he said.

Now Ella wasn't sure if he was apologizing for the mess he'd made or the curse.

"That's all right." She figured the response covered all of the bases.

She set her own glass aside and went to get a dishcloth from the sink. When she returned, Chase surprised her by taking it from her hand and crouching down to scrub the stain himself. She crouched next to him, balancing on the balls of her bare feet.

"It's better to blot it," she told him.

Intending to show him what she meant, Ella reached for the dishcloth. But when her hand touched his and their gazes connected, his expression changed and she swore the air grew charged. She knew that look. She'd seen a couple versions of it on his face already. Once in the elevator right after they met and earlier when she'd opened her apartment door. Those had been tame in comparison. He was interested in more than her party-planning skills. Or lack of them. He wanted to kiss her, possibly more. The thought had a few places on her body starting to tighten and tingle.

The smart thing would have been to push to her feet and pretend she hadn't noticed his interest. Yep, that would have been the smart thing, all right. Except Ella had never been accused of playing it smart, so she leaned forward until their breaths mingled and she could feel the warmth that radiated from his body. On a groan, Chase closed the miniscule gap that remained.

One moment his hands were holding the damp dishrag. The next, the rag was history and his palms were on either side of Ella's face, holding her steady even as his mouth rocked her world. If the man could have that effect with his tongue, she could only imagine what he would be capable of using other parts of his anatomy.

And she'd thought she was over her head when it came to party planning.

The kiss ended. Chase pulled away slowly. Ella blinked, trying to clear her head, and then said the first thing that came to mind.

"Wow."

Okay, so she wasn't exactly articulate when she was turned on.

Chase said nothing. He looked slightly annoyed, whether with her or himself, she couldn't be sure. He placed his hands on his thighs and pushed to his feet. Once he'd risen to his full height, he looked like the no-nonsense, high-powered executive he was.

"I didn't stop by to kiss you."

Ella straightened.

"I didn't think you had." Still, she'd considered it a happy bonus.

But there was nothing "happy" about Chase's expression.

"I don't make it a habit to kiss women I barely know."

How to respond to that? She decided on, "I didn't mind."

He tossed the verbal equivalent of a bucket of ice water in her face when he replied, "But I shouldn't have done it."

"Then why did you?" she asked baldly.

"I…" He shook his head and demanded, "Does my uncle know that you've never planned a party?"

Back to that. Damn. "It hasn't come up."

"Well, that's convenient."

"Hey!" she protested. "*He* called me."

"Only because he received your business card, and on that card it says you are a professional. Yet you have no experience, no specialized training, since I doubt a degree in fashion merchandising counts." He glanced around her apartment and made a scoffing noise. "You don't even have a proper office."

"I could tell you that plenty of people work from home these days. I'm sure a man in your position has heard of telecommuting. I could tell you that what I lack in experience, I make up for in enthusiasm." She folded her arms over her chest, torn between feeling self-conscious and righteously indignant. Indignation won, and so she finished with, "But I'm wondering what I did to tick you off just now."

His eyes widened. Ella doubted many people called Chase Trumbull on the carpet. Or the wine-stained area rug, as the case may be.

"I… You…" He closed his mouth and his lips thinned into a flat line.

She liked them better when they were loose and limber…and on hers.

Since those two sputtered pronouns were all she was likely to get out of him, she continued. "I may be new at planning parties, but I've attended a lot of them. I know what makes for a fun and memorable evening. I know what people like."

"El…Miss Sanborn."

"After that kiss, I think we're on a first-name basis," she told him dryly and had the satisfaction of seeing him flush.

"You have no idea what you've gotten yourself into. Entertaining several hundred guests will not be easy. You can't just tap a few kegs of beer, throw some pretzels into bowls and bring out the board games."

"Gee, and that was my plan." Anger joined ranks with indignation.

"I don't mean to be condescending."

"It's just a side benefit."

His eyes narrowed. "We're talking about a massive undertaking that even a veteran planner would have a hard time coordinating. Caterers, florists, servers, bartenders, tents, tables, chairs, a sound system and entertainment, cleaning services and waste removal." He ticked off a list that, okay, was way more comprehensive than the one Ella already had assembled, before demanding, "What sorts of contacts do you have in these areas?"

"I know some people." Actually, her former stepmother knew those people. Camilla had enjoyed throwing lavish parties while she'd been married to Ella's dad. She still enjoyed throwing those parties, only now a different husband picked up the tab. Ella didn't feel the need to draw the distinction now. But she wanted to leave Chase feeling reassured. "I won't pretend to have all of the answers, but what I don't know I will make it my mission to learn and figure out. I'm very resourceful."

Chase sighed.

"I believe you mean that, Ella." His voice lowered, turned soft. She preferred his anger to patronization, and that's what this was. "But my uncle cannot afford to be your training ground. Too much is at stake right now. He needs someone who knows what she's doing. Not someone who will be learning as she goes."

Ella swallowed. She hated that what he said made sense. What choice did she have but to agree?

"I'll tender my resignation and suggest he find someone else."

Because her eyes had begun to burn with tears, she

turned away from him, forgetting about the glass of wine that she'd set on the floor next to the futon. The coin-size splash of merlot Chase had made on the white rug was nothing in comparison to the crimson tide she'd just unleashed.

"God! This is a mess," she cried.

He found the dishcloth and stepped around her. "It might come out."

She shook her head. "It doesn't matter."

Ella had bigger problems than a ruined rug. She had to return the sizable check Elliot had given her as a deposit, which meant she couldn't pay her rent or catch up on her other bills.

And then there was Chase, the man who had just kissed her with far more passion than she would have guessed lurked beneath such a reserved exterior. Would she see him again? It wasn't likely.

"I'm sorry, Ella. Really." He set down the rag and started for the door.

She waited until she heard it click shut to let her tears fall.

CHAPTER FOUR

CHASE FELT AWFUL. He'd left Ella with a mess on her hands in more ways than one. It was obvious that she needed the income from planning a big party. Even more than that, she needed the experience. One big-name client to use as a reference could make her as a party planner in Manhattan.

If so much weren't on the line, he wouldn't have strong-armed her into quitting. He consoled himself with the fact that she understood his motive. But as consolations went, it was paltry, which was why her defeated expression haunted him that night.

Their kiss in her apartment stayed with him, too.

It wasn't like Chase to mix business with pleasure. And that kiss definitely rated as pleasure. As much as he might wish he would have met Ella Sanborn under different circumstances, there was no denying his interest. Everything about her had him intrigued, starting with her dual eye color and disparate dimples.

She didn't stop by to see Elliot the following day as Chase expected. Or the next. Had she changed her mind? Was she reneging? For that matter, she'd never signed the confidentiality agreement that had been his reason for dropping in on her in the first place. He'd left it in her possession, forgot about it entirely after that kiss.

By Friday night, he gave in to his curiosity and called

her. He had no idea what he would say when she came on the line. That, too, wasn't like him. Chase usually planned ahead and then followed those plans to the letter. He didn't go off half-cocked. That was Uncle Elliot's specialty.

It didn't take a psychology degree to figure out that growing up under Elliot's scattered if loving influence had caused Chase to crave structure, so much so that once he was able to, he'd created it for himself. Some might say he'd gone a little overboard. His modus operandi was to proceed with caution on a well-charted course with a known destination in mind. But he dialed Ella's number anyway and found himself disappointed when he reached her voice mail. He hung up without leaving a message and was replacing the receiver into its cradle in his kitchen when it rang.

"Hello?"

"Hi. This is Ella Sanborn. Someone from this number just tried to call me."

"Ella. Hello. It's Chase Trumbull."

"Oh." Her tone was one of disappointment, an emotion that hit his ego hard. Before he could recover, she was saying, "I'm sorry I haven't been in contact with your uncle yet. I plan to go see him first thing Monday morning. Honest. I would have been in sooner, but I spent some of the deposit he gave me, and I've been waiting until I could give him his money back in full."

Now Chase felt horrible all over again. Ella really needed that money.

"That's not why I was calling," he lied.

"Then why?"

Why indeed.

"I…I…" he stammered, feeling like an idiot as he grasped for a reason. What he came up with was, "I have a job for you."

"A job?" she repeated, clearly surprised.

Well, that made two of them.

"Yes, I, uh, want to throw a…a dinner party," he said when his gaze fell on the takeout menu for his favorite restaurant that was open on the counter.

Chase had a full-size kitchen in the penthouse he'd been subletting since his return from California, one with the kind of appliances that a Cordon Bleu–trained chef would envy. Of course, he had neither the patience nor the time to learn their full range of functions, so most of his meals came courtesy of his favorite restaurants. And when he entertained, which was rare and usually for reasons more business-related than social, he relied on his secretary to see to the details. But Ella could handle it, he thought, warming to the idea. Yes, she could manage coordinating a meal for six or so guests.

"Are you asking me to plan your dinner party? I have no prior experience," she reminded him. "None."

"But you're enthusiastic. You told me so yourself."

"Are you making fun of me?"

"No. I'm hiring you," Chase replied, mind made up.

Ella snorted and sounded far from convinced when she replied, "*You* want to hire *me*. Right."

"I'm serious, Ella."

"Oh, God! This is a pity job, isn't it? You feel sorry for me. That's the only reason you're calling and offering me this opportunity."

Pity. Was that all he felt where Ella was concerned? "Actually, I—"

It was as far as he got before she interjected. "I accept!"

He couldn't help teasing, "Even if it's a pity job?"

"Sure. Beggars, choosers and all that." She was the one doing the teasing when she said, "Let me just step into my office, boot up my computer and you can give me the details."

He pictured ten candy-pink-tipped toes crossing a

stained white rug. "I have a better idea. Can we meet to discuss it in person?"

"I suppose that makes more sense. How about Monday when I stop in to see your uncle?" she suggested.

Monday seemed light years away.

"Actually, I haven't had dinner yet. What about you?"

"An hour ago."

"Oh."

"But I'm always up for dessert."

How could a man not appreciate a woman who would cop to liking dessert? Most of the women he knew were counting calories or carbs or both, and regarded sugar as the devil.

"I know a place that makes the best cheesecake. You like cheesecake, right?"

His question elicited a sound best suited to the bedroom. It was all Chase could do not to moan in response.

"I love it," she said. "Give me the address and tell me what time you want to meet."

The restaurant he had in mind was far closer to his Park Avenue penthouse than her apartment in Lower Manhattan, but he replied, "I thought I would pick you up."

"Okay." She waited a beat. "This is business, right? I mean, it's not a date?"

"Of course it's business," he replied. "Why do you ask?"

He braced himself, fully expecting Ella to mention their kiss, but she said, "Shoe selection. I can be ready in an hour."

"I'll see you then."

After disconnecting, Chase tapped the phone against his chin. Damned if he didn't find himself wondering what kind of shoes she had in mind.

Red stilettos seemed a bit much for a business dinner, even if they were Ella's favorite heels. She put them back in the cupboard and pulled out a pair of purple suede designer pumps. They were the real deal, a gift from her father back when he could still afford to give his daughter outrageously expensive shoes on a whim. Ella hadn't worn them in nearly a year, but the bright plum was just the pop of color the outfit she had in mind needed.

When Chase knocked, she was dressed, shoes on, hair styled and eyes gone smoky thanks to some expertly applied shadow.

"The entrance is propped open again," were the first words out of his mouth when she opened the door.

It wasn't quite the greeting she'd hoped for, but she didn't mind since his eyes then widened fractionally and half of his mouth tipped up.

"I'm ready," she told him.

"So I see."

His gaze still hadn't made it back to her face. Even so, she had just enough vanity to go fishing for a compliment.

"What I'm wearing is suitable, right? You didn't tell me where we were going, so I decided to play it safe and put on a dress."

The other half of his mouth lifted. Ella still wouldn't say he was smiling, but he was clearly pleased.

"You look…perfect."

She'd been going for professional with a heaping side of pretty in the muted yellow print sheath that ended just above her knee, but it was difficult to be disappointed with being called perfect.

"Thanks. You look perfect, too."

And mouthwatering despite being conservative. Did the man own clothing beyond suits? Technically, she supposed, Chase wasn't wearing a suit. Rather, a navy sports jacket and a pair of stone-colored trousers. He wore both exceptionally well. She recognized a tailor's hand when she saw one, but in this case more than gifted stitching was responsible for the fit. The man worked out.

At least he'd left the tie at home. The white button-down was open at the collar. Despite the day's heat, she spied the neckline of a cotton undershirt. At the sight, Ella's mind drifted. She found herself wondering if Chase wore boxers or briefs beneath his pants. Then she found herself wondering what he wore to bed. Most likely pajamas, the cotton plaid variety with a top that buttoned up the front and included a pocket. If she ever got the chance, she would take her time unbuttoning the shirt. Peel off the pants slowly. Boxers or briefs? She didn't care which. When she got to them, she would peel off those slowly, too.

Forget drifting. Her mind had just wandered over a cliff. Sanity followed as she recalled their kiss. She had spent the week trying not to think about it. She hadn't been very successful, even if she'd had bigger issues to concern herself with. Mainly, her lack of income, the mounting stack of bills and coming up with the few hundred bucks of Elliot's deposit that she'd already spent.

"Is something wrong?" Chase's voice sliced through her mind's meanderings.

"Wrong? No."

He nodded. Then, "I have a question for you. It's a little bit personal."

Thong, she nearly said, before pressing her lips together. "Hmm?"

"Why did you go with those shoes?"

Shoes. He would consider that a personal question. She glanced down at the pumps.

"I decided my outfit needed a punch of color."

He nodded, as if he understood, which she doubted. Few men understood a woman's predilection for shoes. Even her former boyfriend, Bradley, who was a clotheshorse himself, had been baffled by her obsession with footwear.

"Ready?" Chase asked.

"Yes."

She retrieved a small clutch from the counter. It was orange, a warm hue that was positioned opposite the purple of her shoes on the color wheel. As such they complemented one another as well as the more neutral-toned dress.

"Aren't you forgetting something?" At her quizzical glance, he added, "A tablet, whether the old-fashioned writing variety or the high-tech kind. You'll need to take notes for my dinner party."

Dinner party. Notes. "Right," she murmured, rummaging through the magazines, correspondence and clothes on her desk. She found a small pad of paper and tucked it into the purse. Then they were on their way. When they passed through the main door downstairs, Chase kicked to the side the brick her neighbor had placed there.

She thought the gesture sweet, even though she knew from prior experience that the guy or one of his bandmates would only put it back.

Ella was familiar with the restaurant Chase chose. It was a favorite of her father's, although it had been a while since either she or Oscar had eaten there. The price of an appetizer could buy her a couple of meals at the places she frequented these days, not that she ate out often. Eating in was much cheaper.

"Mr. Trumbull, so good to see you again," the maître d' said with a hint of a bow. "I must have missed your name on the reservation list."

"You didn't miss it. My guest and I made dinner plans at the last minute. I know it's a Friday night, but I was hoping you could accommodate us."

The man's gaze fell on Ella then and he blinked in surprise. "Miss Sanborn! It's…it's…it's been too long."

She gave him points for the quick recovery as well as diplomacy, even if his complexion paled by several shades.

"Hello, Charles. How are you?"

"I'm well, thank you. And you?"

"Never better," she replied with a smile.

He lowered his voice and glanced around. "Will your father be joining you this evening?"

"No. It's just Chase and me."

The maître d's relief was palpable. Although her heart sank, Ella kept her smile in place.

She didn't need to look at Chase to know he was frowning. Questions were forming. Perhaps he already had answered some of them himself. She hoped any that remained could wait until after she'd eaten a thick slice of The Colton's signature cheesecake, since talking about the past would spoil her appetite.

"Do you think you can find us a table?" she said to Charles.

There had been a time when Ella would have slipped the man a fifty-dollar bill along with the request. Money talked. Her father had taught her how to grease all sorts of skids with various denominations of currency. Now that neither of them had any to spare, doors that once swung wide open were all but bolted shut. That reality, along with the whispered comments whenever he came into a room, had left Oscar Sanborn bitter. Ella considered herself wiser. She put more stock in happiness than prosperity, even if she recognized the need for an income.

"Of course. Right this way."

The table was one of three in a small alcove in the back, secluded from the front of the restaurant. Ella couldn't decide if Charles had seated them there to ensure their privacy or to isolate them from the other guests, her father's reputation being what it was these days.

A waiter appeared almost immediately to take their drink order.

"May I take the liberty of recommending a wine to start, Mr. Trumbull?" he asked.

At Chase's nod, the young man rattled off the selection, touching on its various notes and characteristics.

"I'll defer to the lady," Chase said when the waiter finished. "How does that sound, Ella?"

"I've had the previous year's vintage and did not care for it."

"You will find this one much better."

"All right."

"Bring a half carafe," Chase instructed.

"Excellent, sir." With that, the young man withdrew.

She studied her menu, well aware that Chase was studying her.

"I've changed my mind," she said.

"About?"

"Eating more than dessert. I love their portobello mushrooms. They're grilled and topped with roasted red peppers and goat cheese." She set the menu on the table. "Does that sound all right to you for an appetizer?"

He nodded. "Ella—"

"Can it wait?"

"Can what wait?"

"The inquisition. I know you have questions."

"I do," he agreed on a slow nod. "All right. They can wait."

Chase was true to his word. Of course, she'd expected him to be. Ella had pegged him to be the sort of man who said what he meant and meant what he said. It was a quality she greatly appreciated as she savored the last bite of portobello.

"You should serve these at your dinner party," she suggested, reaching for her wine. "They're a great way to start a meal. Your guests would love them. The Colton does catering. As you must know, their food is always excellent."

"Are they a contact of yours?" He offered one of his almost-smiles.

"I guess they are. In a manner of speaking." She sipped her wine. The waiter had been right about the vintage. It was much better than the label's previous year. When her mind started to wander to the subpar merlot that stained her carpet and the kiss she'd shared with Chase, she decided it was time to get down to business.

"Tell me about this party of yours. Have you decided on a guest list?"

"I…yes."

She narrowed her eyes and asked, "How many people are we talking?"

"I'm thinking…six."

"You just plucked that number out of the air, didn't you?" she accused, regaining her humor. It felt good to laugh.

"Yes."

She gave him points for honesty. "So, does this six include you?"

"Uh, no."

Ella recalled her stepmother's admonitions against uneven numbers at social gatherings. Camilla might have been a back-stabbing bitch, but she knew about such things. "If you are hosting couples, you really should invite a date for yourself. Are…you seeing anyone?"

The question wasn't purely professional. It had nagged at her since that infamous lip-lock earlier in the week.

"I'm not in a relationship, if that's what you mean." He leaned toward her. "I wouldn't have kissed you if I was."

"Good to know." Or was it? As her body began to tingle, she wondered.

Chase turned the question around. "What about you, Ella? Are you involved with anyone?"

"Not recently." Bradley was her last serious boyfriend, and they were ancient history.

"Good."

Those tingles continued when the right side of his mouth quirked up.

"So, will you be inviting a date?" she asked. Since they were awaiting their entrees, she pulled out the notepad and uncapped a pen.

"I don't think so."

"Dinner for seven." She jotted it down.

"Eight." When she glanced up, Chase added. "You're welcome to join us."

"I…" She wasn't sure how to respond. In truth, she wasn't particularly clear on what constituted proper party planner etiquette, but his offer was damned tempting.

"You can make some contacts," Chase went on. "Hand out your business cards."

"That's really nice of you." And, from a purely practical perspective, very appealing. "I'll leave some of my cards with you."

"But you won't stay."

She shook her head. "I may be brand-new at this, but I have a feeling it wouldn't look very professional for me to be both your planner and a guest at your table."

He conceded the point with a nod. From his frown, however, she gathered her answer wasn't what he wanted to hear.

"When are you thinking of hosting this dinner?"

"The sooner the better. I know this is very last minute, but does a week from next Saturday work for you?"

"I didn't bring my appointment calendar with me, but I believe that date is available," she told him dryly.

"I thought it might be." Half of his mouth rose again. "I'll pay you in advance for your services, and you can charge any expenses to my credit card."

Ella nearly wilted in relief at his response. In addition to needing to pay back Elliot, she was down to condiments, half a bag of baby carrots and two cups of Greek yogurt in her fridge.

"I appreciate that. I'll need the names and addresses of your guests. The turnaround will be tight, but I'd like to send out proper invitations rather than rely on email, although to make it easier for your guests they can RSVP via computer."

"I'll get them to you first thing Monday," he replied just as the waiter returned with Chase's steak.

On the table in front of Ella, the waiter placed a plate of mixed baby greens tossed in the house vinaigrette. She'd told Chase the truth about having already eaten, but nibbling on a salad seemed preferable to simply sitting there watching him eat a mouthwatering cut of meat.

Although she put away her notepad, they continued to discuss the dinner party during the meal. He assured her that his dining room and its furnishings could accommodate all of his guests.

"What about place settings, cutlery, stemware and serving pieces? I only ask because not every bachelor has those," she told him.

"I have service for twenty-four."

Her mouth fell open. "Seriously? You have service for twenty-four?"

"Not at the penthouse, but they're packed away in my uncle's attic," he said on a shrug. "They were my mother's."

"Oh. I'm sorry."

Chase frowned in confusion. "Why are you sorry?"

It was Ella's turn to be perplexed. "I...I assumed the fact that you have them now meant she's, well, dead."

Ella had nothing of her late mother's. When Camilla had bailed on Oscar, she'd taken off with her all of the jewelry, trinkets and china that, by rights, should have been Ella's.

Chase was saying, "My mother is very much alive and well. I just haven't seen her in a couple of decades."

Ella blinked. "Sorry," she offered again before she could think better of it. Then she blundered further by saying, "At least you have your dad."

"Actually, my father is dead."

"Oh." It was all she could manage with both of her feet stuffed in her mouth.

Chase took pity on her and changed the subject. "How much wine do you think I should order?"

Grateful for the change in topics, she replied, "I think three bottles should do it for a group that size, unless you are thinking of offering your guests more than one selection to go with the meal."

By the time the waiter had cleared their plates and brought her dessert, Ella had a very good idea of the gathering she would be putting together on Chase's behalf. But that wasn't why she was smiling. The cheesecake looked as good as she remembered with a drizzle of sauce as well as a few fresh strawberries layered on top.

"I'm willing to share," she told Chase.

Unlike her, he had ordered only coffee, which he took black. Ella loved coffee, as long as it came with plenty of cream and a few packets of sweetener.

"That's all right."

"Watching your figure?"

He chuckled. "I think that's supposed to be my line."

"I'm all for role reversal." She tilted her head to one side and smiled. "Well? Do you?"

"Watch my figure?"

"Want a bite."

"Maybe one." He winked. "I can work it off later."

He was talking about exercise. Probably lifting weights or taking a turn on an elliptical machine, but she felt her flesh heat up anyway. She could think of a good way for them both to burn off calories.

Then Ella heard a familiar voice and those first licks of interest were doused as effectively as having a bucket of ice water dumped over her head.

"There are, too, open tables back here, Charles. I don't know what you were thinking, seating us so close to the kitchen," Camilla complained. Then she spied Ella. "Whatever are *you* doing here?"

"Eating a slice of cheesecake." Or she had been. Her appetite was good and ruined now.

Ella's former stepmother was blonder, bustier and more bodacious than she remembered. Of course, Ella had been doing her damnedest to forget the woman.

"Charles, why didn't you mention that Ella was here?"

"An oversight," the maître d' replied, casting an apologetic glance Ella's way.

Camilla continued, "Our relationship may have changed, but there are no hard feelings. Isn't that so, Ella?"

Ella smiled without agreeing. Now was neither the time nor place to air dirty laundry. "You're looking well," she said, determined to be pleasant.

"Thank you. Have you gained a little weight?" Camilla cast a meaningful glance at the cheesecake.

It was the kind of verbal slap Ella expected from the woman who had made her insecure teen years pure hell, and so she was prepared for it.

"Nope. Same weight as before."

"Really? Well, not me. I've lost several pounds. I've been so busy redecorating Javier's villa in Madrid," she said of her new husband.

Javier Saville, plastic surgeon to the rich and famous. Camilla had met him when she'd gone in for a tummy tuck. She appeared to have had a few additional procedures done since then.

"Married life agrees with you," Ella said. And the fact that, these days, Camilla was married to someone other than Ella's father agreed with Ella.

Camilla nodded, before transferring her gaze to Chase. "You'll have to forgive us for being so rude. Ella and I haven't seen one another in…how long has it been?"

"Your divorce from Dad was final two years, six months, three weeks and four, um, no, five days ago." Ella smiled sweetly.

Meanwhile, Camilla's eyes glittered with pure evil. "How is your father, dear? Any more indictments? I wasn't able to follow the news while I was abroad."

"You know damned well he was cleared of all charges," she said between gritted teeth.

"Your table, madam?" Charles inserted in an attempt to keep the situation from escalating. The poor maître d' looked pained. Scenes didn't happen at The Colton.

Camilla ignored him. "That's right. It was all those pesky civil suits from investors who'd lost their life savings that kept him in court."

The burden of proof was lower in civil cases and a couple of sympathetic juries had sided with the plaintiffs. Between legal fees, those settlements and the financial drubbing Oscar had taken in the divorce, he'd wound up nearly broke.

"I'm Chase Trumbull." Chase stood and held out his hand, making it impossible for Camilla to ignore him or continue her not-so-veiled attack on Ella.

"Camilla Saville." Instead of shaking his hand, she gave just the tips of his fingers a light squeeze before adding with an air of importance, "Of the Greenwich, Connecticut, Savilles. Are you and Ella…dating?"

The question was accompanied by a practiced look of surprise.

"Actually, Chase and I are business associates," Ella responded.

"Business associates?" Camilla's lips twisted on the words, before she asked skeptically, "And what business might that be?"

"Ella is a professional party planner."

"Since when?" Camilla snorted indelicately. Chase's icy stare had her offering an apology, albeit an insincere one. "I'm sorry. That came out all wrong. It's just that I'm surprised. The last I heard, and admittedly it was several months ago, Ella was trying her hand at fashion merchandising and not having very much success, I'm afraid."

As if Camilla hadn't gleefully given every contact she knew in the industry an earful.

Chase surprised her by claiming, "Ella is very much in demand. I was lucky to get her, especially on short notice."

Camilla looked as if she wanted to disagree, but couldn't figure out how to do so without making herself appear churlish.

"Trumbull, you said?"

"Of the East Hampton Trumbulls, yes." Even though Chase said it with a straight face, Ella caught the gleam of amusement in his eyes.

Camilla's expression changed to fawning. "East Hampton. Ooh. I adore East Hampton. I've been telling Javier that we should buy a place there. Our penthouse is lovely, but the city can be so tiresome after a while. It would be nice to have a weekend getaway that didn't require a transatlantic flight, if you know what I mean."

"I do."

"You have a place abroad?"

"A chateau in Paris and a Tuscan villa."

Ella didn't know if Chase really owned real estate in Europe, but it didn't matter. Camilla's envy was plain.

"Lovely places."

He nodded. "It was nice to meet you. Now if you'll excuse us, Ella and I have a lot to discuss."

"Of course. Enjoy your dinner."

"Thanks. You, too," Ella said, hoping to put an end to their uncomfortable reunion. If only she had left it there. But no, she had to say, "And tell Bernadette I said hello."

"I will." Camilla lowered her voice. "And may I just say you're taking it well."

"What do you mean?"

"Her engagement."

"Bernadette is engaged? That's wonderful." Even if Ella pitied the poor sap who found himself saddled with her high-maintenance, ill-tempered stepsister.

But Camilla was frowning. "Oh, dear. You don't know, do you?"

"Know what?" Ella asked, fully aware she was going to regret it given the gleam in her former stepmother's eyes.

"Bernadette is marrying Bradley."

CHAPTER FIVE

CHASE ALREADY HAD plenty of questions for Ella. Questions that, at her request, he'd put off asking until after they had finished their meal.

Well, now he had one more.

Who in the hell was Bradley?

Make that two questions. The second being, why should it matter to him?

Chase only knew it did. The guy had to be someone pretty important for Ella's stepmother to fling him in Ella's face the way she had.

Generally speaking, patience wasn't Chase's strong suit, but he exercised what he considered to be an admirable amount while she picked at her cheesecake. With more than half of the slice remaining, she announced she was ready to go. Chase paid for their meal and they left.

He tipped the valet and was buckling his seat belt when Ella said without any prompting, "So, what do you want to know?"

"Am I that obvious?"

"No. But I've had a lot of practice at this."

He didn't ask what "this" she was referring to. Instead, he said, "I'm trying to figure out which question I want you to answer first."

"Let me know when you decide." She turned to look out her window.

"Who are you really?" he blurted out.

She turned to face him, brows beetled. "I'm Ella Sanborn, the newbie party planner you've taken pity on by hiring me to put together a dinner for you the Saturday after next."

"But you're not merely the struggling young woman with the grandiose business dream I first met."

The one who believed in luck and who stopped to pick up stray pennies to enhance her odds. The one who lived in a seedy neighborhood in an apartment that could have been measured in square inches rather than square feet. The one who desperately needed a job.

"Why can't I be that person?" she asked. "Does the fact that I was born wealthy negate my current ambitions?"

Born wealthy. Now they were getting somewhere, even though it was no more than he'd suspected given her taste for fine wines, designer clothes and the fact that she was on a first-name basis with the maître d' at one of the most exclusive restaurants in Manhattan.

Ella was saying, "The person you met the other day, the person you had dinner with tonight, this is who I am. It's who I've always been. *I* haven't changed."

"But your circumstances have, I gather. You've eaten at The Colton before."

"Lots of people have eaten there." She shrugged. "It's open to the public."

Which was true, but the prices on the establishment's menu ensured an affluent clientele, and they both knew it.

"Charles knows you personally, Ella. He asked about your father. And we ran into your stepmother there."

"Former." Ella's voice was surprisingly sharp. "*That* woman is of no relation to me, not even by marriage now.

Thank God!" But then the fight went out of her. "My father is Oscar Sanborn. Perhaps you've heard of him."

Her chin was tilted up in challenge, as if daring Chase to say something negative. Oscar Sanborn. A memory stirred before clicking into place.

"The Wizard of Wall Street. I did a term paper on him while I was at Harvard. His long-term investment strategies were the stuff of legend."

Indeed, the man was considered a financial genius, or had been, until several of his very high-profile clients lost their entire life savings. A couple of last-minute stock sales from his own portfolio kept Oscar Sanborn from going under, as well. Some claimed insider trading, although he was investigated by the feds and cleared of all wrongdoing, but that hadn't stopped the civil suits from being filed. Seventeen in all, only three of which were successful. The last article Chase read about the man noted that he was destitute, divorced and living in seclusion.

It hadn't mentioned a daughter. Much less how drastically her life must have changed as the result of her father's staggering legal difficulties. She would have been in college when her father's business dealings had started to go south. The last of the civil lawsuits had been decided the previous year.

She was a young woman who had been raised in privilege, and as such accustomed to a certain social status and lifestyle. But she wasn't feeling sorry for herself, even though it appeared she had yet to land on her feet.

"I'll have to tell him that," Ella was saying. "He'll be flattered."

"What's he doing these days?" Chase asked casually.

She glanced out her window again. Her tone was overly upbeat when she replied, "Oh, he's retired, but he keeps busy."

Chase could read between the lines. The man who had once ruled Wall Street was now all but a recluse.

"It must have been hard on you. As I recall, his reputation took quite a beating in the press."

Her shoulders lifted. "It was harder on him. People he thought he could count on abandoned him. I think that hurt more than having to defend his business decisions in court or being forced to file bankruptcy."

"Your stepmother," he guessed.

"Camilla was among the first to seek greener pastures... and pocketbooks. Good riddance, I say, even though Dad felt differently. She broke his heart and what was left of his spirit."

"I take it you and Camilla weren't close."

"No. She married my dad not long after my mom died. I tolerated her and her nasty daughter—" the infamous Bernadette, he deduced "—because my father was happy again."

He slowed for a light. "How old were you when they married?"

"I'd just turned eleven." Ella sighed, her tone became wistful. "It's really too bad she was the kind of person she is. I wanted a mother. I missed mine. But right away I recognized Camilla for what she was—a phony and a user."

Chase had his answers. Most of them anyway. He told himself it was none of his business, to leave it be, but he still heard himself asking the question that nagged the most.

"Who's Bradley?"

"Someone I used to date."

He'd gathered that much. And now that someone was marrying Ella's stepsister.

"Was it serious?"

"I thought so at that time." She cleared her throat. When she spoke again, it was to change the subject. "I think I got a good start on plans for your dinner party tonight."

His dinner party. Chase had nearly forgotten about it. "Excellent," he murmured, trying to match her professional tone.

"I'll call The Colton tomorrow and speak to the manager about catering. That is if you think you want to use them."

"Yes."

She nodded. "I'll have them put together a few appetizer, entree and dessert selections, and you can narrow down the menu from there."

They discussed wine for the remainder of the drive. Her familiarity with high-end labels now made perfect sense. Ella had been raised in the same social circles as Chase. If he hadn't moved to California for a time, they very well might have met at some soiree or another. But she was unlike any of the women he knew. A fact that was underscored when they neared her apartment. He couldn't imagine any of them living in this neighborhood much less the shoebox Ella called home. They'd sell their soul first.

"It's a long way down." Her laughter held little mirth.

"Excuse me."

"That's what you're thinking, isn't it? You've seen my apartment. You know that for a while I lived in one even smaller. As you probably guessed, I had a walk-in closet bigger than that in the house where I grew up. So, in that regard, it's a long way down to Lower Manhattan from Central Park West."

Was he really that transparent?

"Remind me to perfect my poker face before the next time I have to deal with the board of directors."

"Speaking of work, I'll be by the Trumbull offices Monday morning. I'll return your uncle's deposit and explain that he needs a more experienced party planner to organize his wake."

"Thank you for understanding."

"And thank you for the pity job." Her smile was impish

and accompanied by those charming dimples. "I wish I had the name of someone I could recommend, but I haven't had need for a party planner in some time. Of course, back when my father hosted large gatherings, Camilla was the one to oversee such details. I trust you will understand when I say I would rather slit my own throat than have to ask her who she used to hire."

It was impossible not to chuckle given Ella's dry tone. It was also impossible not to be impressed with the way she had handled adversity.

They were nearing her apartment. Chase slowed, scanning the street for an open spot near the curb.

"Oh, there's no need to park. Just drop me out front."

"I'll walk you up."

"Seriously, there's no need. Besides, it's impossible to find a place on this block, which is why I don't own a car. Well, that and the fact that I can't afford one at the moment."

The remark might be self-deprecating, but her laughter held no bitterness.

"I can't just leave you at the curb."

"Granted, this isn't one of the better ZIP codes in Manhattan, but, really, this neighborhood's not so bad."

At just that moment, a visibly drunk man shuffled out from an alley, dropped his pants and began to urinate on the lamppost in front of Ella's building.

"You were saying?"

"Oh, for heaven's sake. It's all of five steps to my building's door from the curb. Besides," she continued matter-of-factly, "unlike that lamppost, I'd be a moving target."

At that, a strangled sound escaped Chase. Ella turned and gaped at him.

"Did you just laugh?"

"I…well, you have to admit, what you said was pretty funny. The visual." He shook his head as the image came and chuckled again.

"I like your laugh. You should do it more."

"I haven't had much to laugh about lately," he heard himself admit.

"I laugh at myself. At the silliness of stowing my shoes in kitchen cabinets."

"I admire you for that."

"For my unconventional storage solution?" she asked, but she was grinning. She knew what he meant. "I told you before, I'd rather laugh than cry."

"I remember."

"From your remark about not having much to laugh about, I take it you haven't had any luck getting Elliot to see a doctor."

"No, but I haven't really tried. We've been busy preparing for board meetings and, well, I keep hoping…"

The lump that had formed in his throat kept Chase from going on.

"Try." Ella laid a hand over his on the steering wheel.

Compassion. Comfort. Both came from a woman who could use a little of each herself. He'd never met anyone like her.

It took some doing and a few trips around the block before he found an open spot at the curb just up from her building. Even though the sun had set, the evening remained warm to the point of being uncomfortable. Add in a hot woman and Chase could feel the perspiration gathering on his forehead even before he reached the door, which—no surprise—was held open once more with the brick.

Ella was smiling when his gaze connected with hers.

"Told you," she said.

Though Chase knew it would do little good, he kicked the brick down the sidewalk this time and ushered her inside.

"Are you going to walk me all the way up, too?"

Gallantry warred with self-preservation. As it was, he

wanted to kiss her again, find out if that over-the-top geyser of lust he'd experienced the first time was merely a fluke. If he found himself on her doorstep, her horny neighbor going at it in the hall…. He swallowed.

This wasn't a date. He and Ella were business acquaintances of a sort. He summoned up every ounce of professionalism he possessed.

"I'll leave you here." He took out his phone. "Text me when you get inside your apartment."

"All right." She smiled, whether touched or amused, he couldn't be sure. "I'll see you Monday."

"I'll get those addresses for you." Now, he just had to figure out who to invite, he thought wryly.

"Thank you for dinner."

"An appetizer, a salad and a few forkfuls of cheesecake hardly qualify as dinner."

"Don't forget the wine. It was exceptionally good."

He shrugged. "Even so. Have a good night, Ella."

"Thanks. You, too."

Somehow he doubted a good night was in the cards for him. For as many answers as she'd provided, Chase suddenly had that many more questions.

He was standing in the entrance when he received her text a few minutes later.

"Home. Door bolted. Night."

"Night," he texted back.

Chase was leaving when a guy with a long, scruffy beard and tattoos down both arms called, "Hold the door, dude."

In his hand was the damned brick.

Chase opted for a reasoned approach to start. "Do you live here?"

"Nah, man. Just visiting my buddy up on three."

"The one with the band?"

The guy's lips split in a grin that revealed tobacco-stained teeth. "Yeah. The Waste Haulers. You heard of us?"

"No." Chase would bet he wasn't in the minority on that. "I have a friend who lives on the fourth floor, and I don't appreciate the entrance being propped open to allow just anyone to enter. Know what I mean?"

"Four, huh? You wouldn't happen to be talking about the really hot chick in C, would you?"

The guy's grin had Chase's hands threatening to ball into fists. So much for being reasonable. Chase stepped forward, using his height to his advantage since the other guy was well under six feet.

"I am. And if I see a brick wedged in this door again, whoever put it there will be at the hospital having it surgically removed. Got it?"

Tattoo man backed up a step. "Chill, dude. Like, you seriously need to relax."

People whose opinions Chase valued far more than this man's had told him the same thing. "So, we're clear?"

"Crystal."

The young man went away muttering. Chase, meanwhile, enjoyed a rare smile.

CHAPTER SIX

"BRADLEY IS MARRYING Bernadette?"

Sandra Chesterfield was one of the few people from Ella's old life who hadn't ditched her when the crap over her father hit the fan. They'd been friends since prep school, had nursed one another through the breakup of their favorite boy band, and later held back one another's hair the first time they'd retched from drinking too much at a party. Now *that* was friendship.

"Yes. Camilla was only too happy to pass the news along when I ran into her at The Colton on Friday night."

"Camilla. That woman is such a piece of work." Sandra muttered an epithet before asking, "Are you okay with that?"

"With Bernadette marrying Bradley?" At Sandra's nod, Ella replied, "I am. I was surprised at first. I didn't know they were dating."

"Neither did I, and Cole and I sometimes run into him. Remember all of the nasty remarks Bradley used to make about her behind her back?"

"I do. Which is why once the shock wore off, I found myself doubly relieved that things between the two of us hadn't worked out. He wanted to ensure his social standing more than he wanted to be married. Now that Bernadette's new stepdaddy is so well-connected…." Ella shrugged. "Besides, I did my crying over Bradley a long time ago."

"No lingering feelings?"

"Not even the bad variety," Ella replied on a laugh. "He deserves Bernadette."

"They deserve each other."

The two women were seated on the floor in Ella's apartment, flipping through fashion magazines, sipping iced coffee that Sandra had picked up on her way over, and listening to Motown classics. Or trying to over the thump of the bass and the wail of electric guitar coming from the apartment below hers. Even though it was not yet nine o'clock, the Waste Haulers were already at it. Actually, the band had been at it all night.

"You're smiling again," Sandra remarked. "And I don't think it has anything to do with Bradley deserving to be saddled with Bernadette."

"Just thinking about the guys downstairs." Her grin widened. "Apparently Chase had a word with them about their habit of propping open the entrance. He threatened them with the need for emergency-room services if it happened again."

The lead guitarist had stopped by her apartment late Friday to apologize. His apology had been accompanied by two complimentary tickets to their upcoming gig at a dive bar in the Village. Not that Ella planned to go, but she appreciated the gesture. Both the band's and Chase's. It was nice to have someone looking out for her even if she didn't feel she needed it. One good thing to come out of her father's bankruptcy was that Ella had learned to take care of herself.

"Ah, so that's why the brick was missing when I got here. I like your Chase already."

"He's not *my* Chase. I told you. He's a client."

"A client who took you to The Colton for dinner. Please."

"To discuss business. It was a meeting."

"On a Friday night?"

"I'm self-employed. I set my own hours."

Sandra rolled her eyes. "He picked you up at your apartment, El."

"Which also happens to be my office."

"And dropped you off afterward."

"Same reason."

"He walked you inside."

Ella smiled and sipped her iced coffee. "He's a gentleman."

"He threatened the guys in the band with bodily harm if they didn't stop propping open the door."

"Yeah." She sighed. "He can be really sweet."

"He's sweet, all right. Sweet *on you,*" Sandra persisted. Her friend nodded toward the stain on the rug. "From what you told me about that kiss, I'd say it's only a matter of time before the two of you are tangling up the sheets. I can't wait to meet him. Are you going to bring him to the barbecue?" she asked, referencing her family's huge, annual summertime bash to raise funds for diabetes research.

Ella grew serious. "You're getting ahead of yourself, Sandra."

"How so? Obviously, he's attracted to you."

"Yes," Ella agreed. "And I won't claim it's not mutual, or that I haven't thought of what it would be like to sleep with him." Oh, she'd thought about it, all right. In great detail. "But introductions aren't likely, because this…thing between us isn't going anywhere."

Her friend frowned. "Why not?"

Ella stirred the coffee with her straw before taking a sip. It was with regret that she told her friend, "We're just too different."

"Ever hear of a little thing called opposites attracting?"

"Oh, they attract." Boy, did they ever, in her and Chase's

case. "But they don't stay together. Look at my father and Camilla. Two people couldn't be more different. And we both know how that ended."

"They're a bad example. Your stepmom was a gold digger from the word *go*. They had nothing in common except for money. It's no surprise that when that was gone, so was she."

"Well, Chase and I have nothing in common except a party. Namely, the dinner party I'm planning for him. And the only reason he hired me is because he feels sorry for me."

"Do you really think that's all you have in common or the only reason he hired you?"

Ella shrugged. "I guess we'll find out. Now, I'd better get ready for my appointment to see his uncle. I have a check to return."

A really, really big check.

Ella wore a black gabardine pantsuit. It was the most conservative outfit she owned and would have been positively bland if not for the cut of the jacket, which nipped in at the waist and was cinched by a belt that tied in front. Underneath the jacket, she wore a black camisole that wasn't meant to be seen, but whose lace edges offered back the femininity she felt the outfit stole.

She had purchased the suit to wear to court the day the verdict was read in the last civil case against her father. He'd lost the case and was ordered to repay a staggering sum to the plaintiff. The sober cut and color had been fitting for that, black being associated with mourning. A part of her father had died that day. And it was fitting on this day, too, since she would be telling Elliot that he needed to find someone else to plan his wake.

When she got off the elevator on the seventeenth floor, the reception desk was empty. Owen's and Elliot's offices were closed up tight. The door to Chase's, however, was ajar, so she crossed to it. A peek inside revealed Chase pacing to the window from his desk, his cell phone tucked between his shoulder and his ear as he flipped through some papers.

"You're being shortsighted," he was telling the person on the other end of the line. "Mark my words, you'll regret pulling your support."

He turned and began to pace back to his desk. When he spied Ella, he stopped. "I'll call you back," he said and ended the call.

His expression lost some of its grimness when he waved her inside.

"Good morning," Ella said. "I didn't mean to disturb you. I noticed your door was open and, well, no one else seems to be here today."

"My uncle gave the support staff the day off." Chase sighed. "It's some obscure holiday. Worker Bee Appreciation Day, I believe."

"I see." Her lips twitched. Leave it to Elliot.

Chase, however, wasn't amused. "It's stunts like this that have even the holdouts on the board wanting to defect."

His lips drew into a taut line, giving her the impression he hadn't meant to tell her that. She recalled the confidentiality agreement he'd asked her sign, not that it had been necessary to ensure her silence. Ella had never been the sort to read the tabloids, much less supply them with juicy tidbits of information. That was doubly true now given her father's treatment at their hands.

"I wouldn't call it a stunt. I bet the people who work here are happy to be rewarded for their efforts. And as a businessman, I'm sure you're aware that when morale is good, so is productivity."

"Happy cows give more milk?" he asked.

"I doubt the women who work here would appreciate that analogy," Ella replied dryly.

"Good point."

Half his mouth rose, and some of the worry left his eyes. Because she liked just a little too much knowing that she had the ability to tease him out of a foul mood, she decided to get down to business.

"Do you have something for me?"

"Do I...? Oh, right." He went to his computer, hit a few keys and a moment later the printer on the credenza behind his desk spat out the guest list, complete with addresses, for his dinner party. He handed it to her.

"Thanks." She tucked the papers into her oversize purse. It was periwinkle-blue with a big silver buckle on the front that was more for decoration than anything else. She fiddled with the buckle. "I'll start to work on the invitations and menu right away and get back to you tomorrow."

"All right."

That concluded their business.

"Is Elliot here?"

"No, but he should be in shortly. He and Owen attended a breakfast for a children's charity this morning."

"Oh. I'll just wait in the reception area, then." She backed up a step, but before she could turn, Chase said, "You look...different today."

"Different good or different bad," she asked, since different wasn't necessarily a compliment.

He leaned a hip against the edge of his desk and folded his arms across his chest. "Different conservative."

"Oh." She plucked at the lapel of the no-frills blazer and admitted, "This isn't my best look."

"I didn't say that. But now you've got me curious. If you don't think you look good in that outfit, why did you wear it?"

Ella thought it best not to mention her thoughts on

mourning. Instead, she replied, "It seemed appropriate for the workplace."

He nodded as his gaze meandered down from her face. "Black isn't your color. You need something more vibrant to go with your personality. But I like the bow." He motioned to the belt.

Her fingers left the lapel to fiddle with one of the loops. "It's the only thing that keeps the outfit from being truly boring."

"That and the shoes." Half his mouth lifted again, but it was more than humor she saw in his eyes now.

"You like?"

Ella set her bag on a chair and then shifted her weight to her left hip so she could position the right one in front of her. The nude, peep-toe pump would have been as sedate as the suit if not for the silver studs dotting it. When they caught the light, they all but shouted *va-va-va-voom!*

"I like." Chase agreed. When he stepped closer, his gaze was no longer on her footwear.

Ella's heart stuttered in her chest.

Is he going to kiss me again?

She answered the question herself. "I'm not going to wait to find out."

"Excuse me?" Chase said.

"Never mind." She laughed. And then, since the man stood within easy reach, she grabbed the lapels of his suit coat and hauled him closer for a kiss.

He blinked in surprise when her lips met his, but then his hands clamped on to her waist and she felt his fingers dig in to her flesh through the suit's gabardine as he pulled her closer. That, as much as the low groan that emanated from the back of his throat, told her he was as turned on as she was. Ella closed her eyes and gave herself over to the moment.

The kiss didn't end so much as it morphed into something else. Namely, a shiver-worthy exploration of her jaw by his mouth. When Chase pushed back her hair and started on her neck, she tilted her head sideways, only too eager to allow him greater access.

"I'm wondering something," he murmured against her throat.

She knew a moment of triumph that his breathing was as ragged as hers. It would really suck if she were the only who felt as if she might explode.

"What might that be?" she asked.

"What do you have on under this jacket?"

Tha-tha-thunk! Tha-tha-thunk! Her heart pounded as she told him, "Why don't you find out?"

Laughter—rich, low and deliciously male—rumbled in response. It vibrated through her body along with an insane amount of need. It was all Ella could do to keep from screaming out, "Yes!" when she felt a tug at her waist and the belt went slack.

Their surroundings faded into oblivion. Everything faded, so that what stood out in stark relief was a need as basic and essential as breathing.

Chase whistled as he peeled back the jacket, which rested on her shoulders only briefly before slipping down her arms and falling to the floor. Neither of them made any move to retrieve it. The jacket was as forgotten as their surroundings.

"This cami is a little plain. But the lace is enough to make me look and feel like a girl despite the boring suit."

He made a humming sound. "I'll say."

She glanced down to find both of her nipples standing at attention, straining against the silk. Chase brushed the backs of his knuckles across one before placing his mouth over it through the fabric. Ella moaned and glanced askance at his desktop. Clear off the blotter and it would do in a pinch. So would the floor. Heck, even a wall…

The ding of the elevator, along with Chase's uttered expletive, breached the haze of her hormones. Someone was coming.

Both she and Chase reached down at the same time to retrieve her jacket from the floor. Their foreheads smacked together with enough force that she saw stars.

"God. Sorry." He held Ella's jacket so she could slip into it. "Are you hurt?"

"Nah. Slight concussion maybe. You?"

"Same," he replied.

She'd just finished tying the belt when Elliot poked his head in the office. His eyes lit up when he saw her. "Isabella, my dear. You look even lovelier than I remember. God, how I've missed you."

"I'm Ella," she corrected gently. "Ella Sanborn."

A knot formed in her throat at his confused expression.

"Isabella was his wife," Chase whispered, his expression forlorn.

Owen came into view then. He'd heard the exchange, too.

"Ella, hello." Owen's tone was gentle when he told his father, "You hired her to plan your party, remember?"

"Party?"

"Wake." Chase supplied.

"Right. My wake. Exactly." Elliot nodded vigorously, his gaze once again focused. "You're here to discuss the plans."

"Yes. Why don't we go to your office?" Her gaze slid briefly to Chase as she started for the door. "What you have in mind is very large and will require a lot of expertise to carry off. I've been doing some thinking…"

That was all Chase was privy to before he heard Elliot's door close. Alone in his own office, he sank down in the leather chair behind his desk, thankful to be alone. He needed a few minutes of privacy to collect his thoughts and get both his breathing and his body under control.

This was a place of business, not a hotel room, but if not for Owen and Elliot's untimely interruption, Chase couldn't say for certain that things with Ella wouldn't have progressed to their logical conclusion.

That thought had him scrubbing a hand over his face. There was nothing logical about having sex in his office with the door half open. He'd fired people for less egregious breaches of professionalism. But damned if he wasn't still as turned on as all hell when he glanced to where Ella had stood minutes earlier, her top discarded along with his own good intentions.

She deserved better than that.

Half an hour later, when he heard her voice outside his office, he felt composed enough to join her and his uncle in the reception area. Owen was there, too.

"Did everything get sorted out?" he asked Ella.

"It…did."

"Good." It really was for the best that his uncle's huge undertaking would soon be in more capable hands. "I took the liberty of compiling a list of more established party planners," he told his uncle. It included some of the city's most elite and well-respected services. He didn't mention that he'd also drawn up contract specifications and confidentiality agreements for whoever eventually landed the job.

"That's very thoughtful of you, Chase," Elliot began. "But Ella—"

"I know what you're thinking," he interrupted. "Ella deserves some compensation for the time that she's put in already. I think letting her keep the deposit would be reasonable." Indeed, he should have thought of that earlier. "And, I don't know if she mentioned it, but I've asked her to plan a small party for me at the penthouse."

"Really?" Elliot blinked at that. "She didn't tell me." His grin unfurled. "So, you're throwing a party?"

His uncle's surprise troubled Chase. Was he really seen as such a stick in the mud that throwing a party would be out of the realm of possibilities?

"It's dinner for six. Well, seven including Chase," Ella supplied.

"Oh." Elliot's expression deflated like a beach ball that had sprung a leak. "That's not really the same as a party."

Chase caught himself before he could argue. They were getting off track—something that was easy to do when conversing with his uncle.

"The point is Ella needs more experience when it comes to her new line of work, and she'll be getting it."

"How practical of you, Chase," Owen drawled, eyes gleaming. "Saint Chase. Always willing to help out the little man. Or woman, in this case."

"It is practical," he said.

"He's doing it as a favor, really." Ella smiled.

Chase nodded, glad that she saw it that way. The dinner party would allow her to get her feet wet on a much more manageable event. That was much better than having her foundering right out of the starting gate while trying to plan a party for seven hundred. A party that would see more than its fair share of media coverage.

Elliot nodded, too. "Good thinking, my boy. I'm on the guest list for your dinner, I assume."

"Uh, actually—"

"I'm eager to see Ella in action," Elliot said.

Okay, it would be dinner for eight. Rounding up the number shouldn't pose a problem at this stage. He'd only just given Ella the addresses.

"It will give me an idea of what to expect," his uncle continued.

"Expect?"

"For the wake."

"Wh-what?" Chase's gaze cut to Ella, who smiled sheepishly before glancing away.

"He wouldn't let me quit, even after I explained that I am brand-new to the business," she mumbled.

"All of us were new at our jobs at one time or another. That's what Dad told her," Owen inserted with a told-you-so smile.

"Quite right," Elliot agreed.

"But Ella's background is in *fashion merchandising.*"

For a moment, the scene with Camilla at The Colton played back. Chase had defended Ella then every bit as vigorously as he was denouncing her abilities now. That was different, he assured himself, even as the word *hypocrite* whispered in his head.

Elliot waved his hand in dismissive fashion. "I don't care what her background is or even if she has a college degree. I never graduated from high school. I earned a general equivalency degree later on, but, sadly, I found school boring at the time."

Chase tried again. "But making toys, Uncle, it was and remains your passion. Party planning is, well, something that Ella is just dabbling in."

"I'm not dabbling." She frowned at him, her expression wounded. "This is what I want to do."

"See?" Elliot looked pleased. "When I created the prototype for Randy the Robot, the established toy companies wouldn't give me the time of day. It's why I decided to launch my own. Everyone deserves a chance. I'm giving Ella hers."

"It's settled, Chase. Why not accept it?" Owen added with double meaning. "Dad is going to get his Irish wake. The media will be there. The board of directors will be in attendance. And Ella is in charge of it."

Owen smiled.

Chase swore.

CHAPTER SEVEN

"You're angry," Ella said.

"You're right."

They were in the elevator heading to the lobby. Chase still had sixteen more floors during which he could vent, but to Ella's surprise that was all he said on the subject. Instead, he pulled out his cell phone, punched in a number and barked, "Bring my car around," to whoever had the misfortune of being on the other end of the line.

At street level, he escorted her to the main doors. She half expected him to toss her out on her rear, given the murder lurking in his eyes and the way his jaw tightened. Instead, he held open the door for her and then followed her outside.

"Are you going somewhere?" she asked as they stood on the sidewalk.

"Besides insane, you mean?"

"You don't need to leave the building for that," Ella pointed out with a grin that earned her a withering glare.

"I've decided to take a short break." He glanced up the street, apparently searching for the car he'd ordered brought around.

She raised her hand to hail a cab, but he stopped her.

"What are you doing?" she asked as his fingers wove through hers and he held on.

"You're coming with me."

Ella blinked. "Where are we going?"

"My place."

"You want to take me home with you?"

Their sexy antics in Chase's office prior to his uncle and cousin's arrival blasted through her mind. His home would afford both privacy and a flat surface more conducive to lovemaking. But Chase's current mood seemed all wrong for romance.

"You can check out the dining room and configure the place settings for my dinner party."

He had a flat surface in mind, all right. But it wasn't the one she was thinking of. She should have been relieved that Chase still wanted her for the job. More than ever, she needed the experience it offered. But the request caught her off guard. He hadn't mentioned it earlier. Of course, he hadn't mentioned a lot of things since both of their mouths had been put to more satisfying uses than conversation.

"N-now?" she sputtered.

"What? You can't spare a few minutes before you start on the plans for my uncle's wake?" he drawled.

"That's not fair."

"Fair!" Anger flashed in his eyes. "You agreed to quit, Ella."

"I tried!" And she had, but ultimately Elliot had been adamant that she stay on. He had faith in her abilities, he'd told her. And, damn, if hearing that hadn't made her want to tackle the job all the more. Still, she resented Chase's implication that she'd somehow gone behind his back. "I made it perfectly clear to your uncle that I didn't have any experience, but Elliot was adamant. Owen agreed."

"Owen?" Chase's eyes narrowed.

She swallowed and admitted, "Elliot asked him what he thought and he said I was perfect for the job."

"I should have known," Chase muttered. "What else did my cousin say?"

"Not much." She scuffed the toe of one blinged-out shoe on the pavement. "Just that he agreed with Madame Maroushka."

"Madame—who in the hell is Madame Maroushka?"

Ella winced at his tone. She hadn't planned to mention the fortune-teller to Chase, even though she'd told Elliot and Owen about her visit to the woman as a way to illustrate why she wasn't right for the job. She might have known that Elliot would see her avant-garde approach to finding gainful employment as a plus. She doubted Chase would agree. Well, the cat was out of the bag now. No reason to try to stuff it back in. Besides, it wasn't as if the man could become more irritated with her. Based on his expression, he was already well past the point of being irate.

Ella's spine stiffened. Come to think of it, she was starting to feel a little ticked off herself. She was being made to feel like the bad guy in this situation when technically none of it was her fault.

So, summoning up an air of nonchalance, she informed Chase, "Madame Maroushka is a fortune-teller. When I paid her to read my palm last month, she told me that she saw me planning parties for a living."

Chase let slip the mother of all expletives in a voice loud enough that some of the pedestrians marching past them on the sidewalk turned and glared disapprovingly.

"*That's* how you became a party planner?" he asked, incredulous.

"Yes." Ella notched up her chin. "I bought business cards that very day. I've been looking for a full-time job in my field since graduation without any luck." She briefly explained to him about Camilla. "This seemed like a viable alternative."

"Perfect. You live in a shoebox of an apartment in a

building populated by miscreants and nymphomaniacs in a neighborhood where drunks mistake lampposts for urinals and you make a major career decision based on the advice of a palm reader." He cursed again, this time with less verve and volume. "And people think my uncle is the one with a screw loose."

"Okay, my approach might be a little unconventional," she began.

"No. Wearing those shoes to a business meeting is unconventional. Listening to a con artist—"

"Palm reader," she interjected.

Chase nodded. "Like I said, listening to a *con artist* is frigging nuts. She probably got a kickback from the guy who printed up your business cards."

"She did not." When Chase stared at her, brows raised, Ella admitted. "Okay, he's her nephew and she tried to fix us up, but she wasn't getting any money for referring me to him. In fact, she gave me a coupon."

He scrubbed a hand over his face. "Ella, do you really think someone can look at the lines on your hand and accurately predict the future?"

She shrugged. "She saw me at a party."

"Let me guess, since she knew you were single, she also saw you with a man. Am I right?"

Ella didn't care for the direction their conversation was taking. She folded her arms over her chest and muttered, "Madame Maroushka may have mentioned a man."

She'd said he was tall and handsome. But not dark. Fair. Like Chase. Hmm. Gooseflesh threatened to prickle Ella's arms. She studied Chase a moment before adding, "Of course, she didn't tell me he'd have such a bad attitude."

He snorted. "Maybe she was referring to someone else."

"Maybe she was referring to your cousin. Owen said Madame Maroushka was right, and that I'd found my calling."

Thunderclouds had nothing on Chase's ominous expression. "You'd be smart not to put stock in anything my cousin says. He's a shameless flirt, whether in the office or out."

Happy to have someone other than herself to discuss, she said, "Is that why the two of you don't get along?"

"It goes beyond that." Chase rubbed his eyes and sighed. Some of the fight went out of him. "He has a permanent chip on his shoulder."

Before she could ask why, the car arrived. The man behind the wheel hopped out as Chase opened the passenger door for Ella. He was angry with her, but he hadn't forgotten his manners.

Well, not completely, she amended, when he snapped, "Are you coming or what? I don't have all day."

"And here I was just thinking how well-mannered you are, despite being upset."

He closed his eyes briefly. "Can you *please* get in the car, Ella? We have things to discuss."

She decided to cut him some slack. He was right about having things to discuss. Just as he was right about her being in over her head when it came to Elliot's party. But what was she going to do? Returning to the palm reader for advice was out of the question.

So Ella got in the car, folded her hands in her lap and crossed her ankles demurely. She kept her gaze glued to the shoes he'd labeled unconventional for the duration of the drive.

It came as no surprise that Chase lived in one of Manhattan's most exclusive ZIP codes. Or that his building boasted snazzily dressed doormen and a keen-eyed guard who sat perched behind a security desk. Nor was Ella surprised when they boarded an elevator that required a special key to access his apartment. It whisked them to the top floor.

Only the penthouse would do for someone with Chase's discerning taste.

Ella supposed a lot of women would have been impressed with his exclusive address, not to mention the breathtaking view of the city that was visible from the windows in his living room. But she'd once lived in a place every bit as prestigious, with a view of the Hudson that had sent real estate agents into a swoon as they'd calculated their potential commission upon sale.

The address didn't make the man. Or the woman, she liked to think. People made themselves. Right now, unfortunately, all Ella had managed to make was a mess.

"The dining room is through here," Chase said.

He tossed his keys onto the foyer's console table, where they slid across the polished surface before falling to the floor with a clatter. Chase swore softly as he stooped to pick them up. Even so, he didn't appear quite so angry now. She might not know him very well, but she saw frustration in the set of his mouth, anxiety in the crease of his brow. He was worried about his uncle. Ella's heart squeezed. She caught his arm as he moved passed her.

"Before we start on business, can we talk about, well, business? I don't want to make things worse for Elliot, Chase. Honest. I may not know him well, but it's not hard to adore him, and I don't want to do anything to jeopardize his position at Trumbull."

He sighed. "I know. I'm sorry."

"I can try to quit again," she offered. "Maybe I should call him and resign over the phone, or pick a time when Owen won't be around to agree with him."

"Owen." He spat out the name.

Curiosity once again piqued, she said, "You mentioned earlier that he has a chip on his shoulder where you're concerned."

She left it at that, waiting for Chase to either tell her it was none of her business or fill in the blank. It took a moment, but finally he did the latter.

"Elliot and my Aunt Isabella raised me after my father died, so Owen and I grew up together. Owen resented my intrusion both in his life and his household."

"How old were you at the time?"

"I was ten. Owen eight."

"That's a hard age," she murmured, thinking of her own adolescence and how she'd felt when Camilla married her father and Bernadette moved in. "No child likes to have to share the affection of a parent with someone else."

"I didn't *ask* for Elliot's affection, much less to become the favorite." Chase shook his head and sighed. "The older Owen and I got, the more competitive he became, and the more my uncle drew comparisons between the two of us."

"Uh-oh."

"Yeah. It wasn't fair to Owen. Even as a kid, I saw that."

"Did you ever try to talk to Elliot? Explain how you felt and how Owen must have felt?"

"I did. So did my aunt. Owen and I were in high school by then. Elliot was proud of me for taking first place at the science fair. Owen earned second in his grade. We went out to eat after the awards presentation. Elliot made a big deal over my win. Owen, meanwhile, sulked through the meal. I told my uncle afterward that I thought Owen was being short-changed, by Elliot and even the awards committee.

"He made this really cool voice-activated light. In a lot of ways, he's like Elliot. Very curious and creative. Meanwhile, I did this rather boring report on allelopathy."

"Allelo-huh?"

"Some plants, like sweet potatoes, release chemicals that inhibit the growth of other plants near them."

"Okaaaay."

"Your eyes glazed over, but the judges loved it," Chase said wryly. "Anyway, I told Elliot that Owen's project showed a lot more ingenuity than mine, and that I thought the only reason he didn't get first place was because they probably thought he'd had help from Elliot. Unfortunately, that only made things worse."

"How so?"

"Owen somehow got wind of my remarks and he confronted me later that night. He basically told me he would earn his father's approval on his own. He didn't appreciate my interference. We got into a fight."

"A fight fight?"

"If you mean fistfight, yes." He rubbed his jaw, as if remembering a blow. "I was only defending myself, but he wound up with a black eye."

"What did Elliot say?"

"He was in his own little world much of the time. I doubt he noticed." Chase sighed. "My aunt tried to comfort Owen, but that just ticked him off more."

"It's not your fault," Ella said softly.

Chase shrugged. "Maybe not, but I wish things could have been different between us. After college, I left New York. Elliot had a position for me here, but I chose to work at the Trumbull offices in California."

Ella's heart squeezed. Chase had put an entire country between himself and Owen. Not just Owen, but the only family he had.

"You didn't want to stand in Owen's way. That's admirable."

"Yet here I am."

"You must have had a good reason for coming back."

"Elliot asked me to. Eighteen months ago. My aunt was gone and… That was when his problems with forgetfulness started becoming really noticeable. So, I put my life in California on hold, leased this penthouse," he added with a wave of his arms.

An alarm bell sounded in Ella's head. He'd said that his

life in California was on hold, which implied that eventually he would return to it.

He was saying, "I felt I had to return. Just after the economy tanked, the company started to founder. It was family-owned then." He shook his head. His expression was not only grim, but guilty when he told her, "It was my bright idea to take it public several years back. Believe me, if I could do it over again…"

Ella shoved her own concerns aside. "It may have been your idea, Chase, but you had to have your uncle's support in order to do it. And you couldn't have predicted the economy's utter collapse."

He studied her. Just about the time she became uncomfortable, he surprised her by saying, "Thank you, Ella."

"For what?"

"For trying to make me feel better."

"Is it working?"

Half of his mouth rose. "Maybe a little."

"You're welcome then." She smiled

His gaze cut to her lips and she swore the temperature in the room shot up a dozen degrees.

"Dining room," he said with a decisive nod and turned quickly on his heel.

His stride was long and purposeful as he maneuvered through a living room whose furnishings were clean-lined and contemporary in style. Along the way, he ditched his suit coat, which he tossed over the back of the sofa. His dress shirt fit snug over his shoulders and tapered at the waist before disappearing into dark trousers. *Mmm.* Nice rear view.

"What do you think?" he asked as they arrived at their destination.

What did she think? Now there was a loaded question given the inappropriate images that were popping around in her head like heated kernels of corn. She paced to the other side of the room and concentrated on the decor.

"Nice table." Large. Flat. Handy.

"I can put in another leaf," he said.

"I don't know that you'll need to. It's expansive even without it." She ran her hand over the edge of the dark wood, as her body hummed with need. It could easily accommodate them.

"What about the sideboard?" He motioned behind her.

She turned and gave it the once-over. The piece sported the same dark stain and clean lines as the table, but it was topped in white marble streaked with gray veins, making it a much harder and colder surface than the table. Still...

"It's a good height." In fact, if Ella were to sit on its edge, Chase's mouth would be level with... She closed her eyes briefly. "Perfect."

"Yeah? What will you use it for?"

She felt heat flood into her cheeks, as well as other parts of her anatomy, and fought the urge to fan herself as she stammered, "W-well, um, let's see…"

"Appetizers?" he suggested.

"Sure. Appetizers." She nodded.

"Or maybe it would be good for cocktails. I can put out bottles of liquor and mixers and my guests can serve themselves prior to the meal. What do you think?"

She was expected to think? Eyes glued to the marble top, she managed to say, "That would be another excellent use."

"But you have something else in mind. I can tell."

"I, um…" Her gaze cut back to Chase then, taking in broody eyes, lean cheeks and a mouth that, as far as she was concerned, should be registered as a lethal weapon. Despite the unruly cowlick, his sandy hair was impossibly neat. His shoulders were broad, and accented in a white dress shirt whose crisp cotton was divided down the middle by a length of navy-and-red-striped silk.

"I…I…"

"Go on. Be honest, Ella."

"I'm not sure that's a good idea," she murmured and a husky laugh rumbled out.

"Tell me."

She waited a beat, almost hoping the words in her head weren't the ones that would slip from her tongue. No such luck, she realized, but without too much regret, when she heard herself tell him, "I'd like you to lose your tie."

Chase's mouth fell open momentarily before he managed a response. "What did you just say?"

They had already established that Ella was unconventional and perhaps even a bit of a kook. So, what the hell?

"The tie. I want you to take it off." She shrugged. "You told me I could be honest."

"I meant about my dining room."

"But that's not why you brought me here."

He shook his head as if to clear it. "What are you talking about?"

"You." She winked. "And me." This time she bobbed her eyebrows.

He made a series of incoherent sounds that served as his reply. She doubted someone as cool and collected as Chase Trumbull was ever quite so inarticulate with other people.

Score one for me.

"In your office earlier today, before you got all pissy with me." She sent him a grin. "Which I forgive you for, by the way—"

"You—"

"Forgive you. Yes."

She wasn't sure why she was pushing Chase, or, for that matter, why she was pursuing him in such a bold fashion. It wasn't like her to be this assertive when it came to men. As a result, from high school on, Ella had found herself in a long-term relationship with Bradley, the perfect match in everyone's opinion except her own. Since their breakup, she hadn't dated much. She'd been too busy trying to cobble together a new life for herself, and trying, albeit unsuccessfully, to help her father find his footing, both financially and emotionally.

But the men she had gone out with had been totally wrong for her. Or married, in the case of the jerk who'd neglected to mention he had a knitting-needle-wielding wife.

Chase probably was all wrong for her, too. As Ella had told Sandra, the two of them had nothing in common except a party and a boatload of sexual chemistry.

That wasn't quite true, she amended. They both had lost a parent. And they both had grown up in a household with another quasi-sibling, who'd made their life difficult.

Her reasonable self told her turned-on self to stop, given what he'd just said about California and his life there. A life to which he apparently would return. But she didn't care. Right now, she wanted to feel the burn. The fallout…she'd deal with that another time.

"Ella, I'm very attracted to you, but I brought you here for business. I don't…I don't mix business with pleasure."

She called him out on that. "Really? When we were back in your office, are you saying that I imagined your mouth on my b—"

"No! But I'm not like Owen. That sort of…behavior doesn't belong in the workplace."

"It's not an ideal setting. Too many disruptions. Not enough practical flat surfaces," she finished, feeling emboldened when a glance down revealed that Chase's body was in agreement with her.

"Yes." He cleared his throat. "I mean, that's not the point I am trying to make."

If they were talking about points, Ella decided she'd scored another one, because his gaze had now drifted from her eyes to her mouth. It settled there briefly before heading to the V where her jacket came together. Was he remembering the moment when he'd peeled it back? She certainly was.

"We're not in your workplace now," she told him.

His gaze snapped back to hers. "Technically, we're in yours." He cleared his throat. "What are your thoughts on workplace fraternization?"

Ella smiled. "I'm all for it, as long as both parties are in agreement. So?"

His hand moved to his tie. He loosened the knot and pulled it away from his collar.

"Is that your answer?"

He smiled. Full-on. Her heart skipped several beats only to make up the difference a moment later when he added, "Your turn. The jacket. Take it off."

"Are you sure you don't want to? You did a pretty good job undressing me in your office."

His eyes lit up at the mention of that. "I'd rather watch you do it this time."

"All right." She did as he commanded, moving with excruciating slowness. Afterward, Ella reached for him. "Now, let me tell you what I have in mind for your sideboard."

CHAPTER EIGHT

SEX COMPLICATED THINGS. Chase had never been in a relationship with a woman when it hadn't. So he was a little surprised that after a few hours of indulging in the mind-blowing variety with Ella, she hopped up from the bed—they'd eventually made it out of the dining room—and announced that she had to be going.

No clinging. No covert glances. No asking when he would call or even if. The only question she posed was, "Any idea where I left my panties?"

Like he was supposed to remember something like that? Hell, Chase figured he was doing pretty well to recall his own name in the afterglow of some of the best sex he'd ever had. Still, he swung his legs over the side of the mattress and stood, pulling on a pair of clean boxers before he followed her out of the room. He was game to help Ella look for her panties, especially if it meant he got to watch her walk around the penthouse wearing nothing but her black cami and a satisfied smile.

They came across her jacket slung across a chair in the dining room where she'd peeled it off at his command. Her pants were in a heap on the floor next to the sideboard, along with her sexy heels, his wingtips and most of his clothing. As for her panties, however, even a thorough search failed to turn them up.

Not that he was complaining.

"The waist will be big, but you can borrow a pair of my boxers," he offered, growing hard just thinking about the way Ella's curves would fill out the checkered cotton.

"Thanks, but I'll pass." She glanced at her watch and grimaced. "I won't have enough time to stop at my apartment. I guess I'll have to go commando."

She stepped into the pants and began pulling them up. Odd, but Chase found watching her dress almost as much of a turn-on as watching her disrobe. She put on shoes next, her movements deft and decisive even as he was having second thoughts about letting her leave. He had to get back to the office. He'd been away too long already. But…

"Where are you off to in such a hurry?" he asked, managing to sound casual despite his mounting curiosity.

"I'm meeting my father to look at an apartment, and then we're going to have an early dinner." She smiled then, mismatched eyes lighting up with pride. "My treat, now that I'm gainfully employed."

"Are you moving?" Chase asked.

God, he hoped so. He really didn't like her neighborhood or her apartment building, even if he was pretty sure that he'd solved the brick-as-doorstop issue with the downstairs neighbors.

"No. My father is. He's been staying at a friend's condo on Long Island since…" The corners of her mouth turned down briefly. "Anyway, his friend wants to lease it out now, so Dad needs to find a new place."

Left unsaid was that her father couldn't afford the condo's rent.

"So, where's he looking?"

"Brooklyn. There's a decent-size walkup that his real estate agent says comes partially furnished. It's close to a grocery store and public transit. I'm not familiar with the neighborhood, but the place sounds pretty nice."

The place sounded like a huge step down from Oscar's previous address, although probably not as far down as her studio in Lower Manhattan was, but Chase didn't say so. Instead, he asked, "What time do you think you'll be home tonight?"

Ella had been tying the belt on her jacket. She stopped, glanced up. "Why?"

Why indeed. It was none of his business, even if they just had engaged in amazing sex.

Chase shrugged. "No reason. I was just wondering."

"If you're worried about the invitations to your dinner party, I'm planning to address and hand-deliver them first thing in the morning."

His dinner party and, more importantly, his uncle's wake. Those were what Chase should be concerned about right now, not whether Ella got home safely. Or what she would be wearing when she finally went to bed that night.

"Excellent. And the menu?"

"I'll call you tomorrow after I speak with the manager at The Colton."

As he walked her back through the penthouse to the elevator, awkwardness settled in. Chase prided himself on always knowing what to say, whether to a woman with whom he'd just made love or a business rival eager to thwart Trumbull's bottom line. But he was tongue-tied now and felt oddly conspicuous.

At the elevator, he blurted out, "Thanks."

Ella eyed him, her expression puzzled, and no wonder. Thanks? It wasn't exactly what a woman expected to hear as she left a guy's place after brain-scrambling sex.

"Um, for coming." His double-entendre of a clarification made things worse.

Chase went to tuck his hands into his pockets, only to realize he wasn't wearing pants. He settled them on his waist instead, just above the logoed band of his boxers.

He was searching for a way to restore his cool and salvage the situation when her mouth curved with a satisfied grin.

"That was entirely my pleasure."

She leaned in and gave him a kiss before boarding the elevator. "I'll be in touch tomorrow," she promised.

After the doors closed, Chase found himself smiling, too. Damned if he wasn't looking forward to her call.

Which made his conscience prick when he found the list of seasoned party planners he'd compiled for his uncle and dialed the number of the one at the top. As much as he wanted Ella to succeed at her new venture, he couldn't take any chances. His uncle had hired her and was determined to keep her on, but that didn't mean Chase couldn't pay for the advice of a real professional and surreptitiously feed it to Ella as needed.

Ella unscrewed the lid on a jar of peanut butter and scooped out a spoonful, which she drizzled with chocolate syrup before putting it in her mouth.

The treat was high in calories, but relatively low in cost. When she'd no longer been able to afford her favorite imported Belgium chocolates, she'd come up with this and other creative ways to indulge her sweet tooth. She gave the spoon a final lick before placing it in the sink next to her coffee cup and cereal bowl. Even something simple could be satisfying.

What was going on with Chase was a case in point. It was sex, pure and simple. Okay, with a side of work thrown in. But it wasn't a relationship. As long as she kept that in mind, everything would be fine. And fun.

As Ella had told Madame Maroushka, she wasn't looking for a man. She was after gainful employment, something that would pay her bills and maybe offer some personal satisfaction. Eventually, a position would open up in her chosen field. Fashion, after all, was her passion.

Or was it?

A little voice whispered that maybe she'd found a new passion. Unsure whether it was referring to party planning or Chase, Ella chose to ignore it.

If only she could ignore the ache around her heart where her father was concerned. She sighed, recalling the time they'd spent together the previous day. It had started with his disapproval over her choice in outfits, and gone downhill from there.

Ella hadn't planned to meet her father wearing the suit, given its negative association. Of course, neither had she planned to spend three hours in Chase's apartment exploring his body and trying not to moan too loudly while he discovered new erogenous zones on hers.

Chase. *Mmm.*

Ella tipped her head back and squirted some chocolate syrup directly onto her tongue. Unfortunately, neither the syrup nor memories of the yummy man could eradicate the sour taste that spending time with her dad had left in her mouth.

By the end of the visit, she'd wanted to give her father a good shake, tell him to get over it already, to move on and man up. She'd stayed silent, despite Oscar's comments about her new career. He was embarrassed that she could wind up planning parties for the sort of people whose homes they had once been invited into as guests. Worse, when she'd told him about Elliot Trumbull's bash, he'd expressed doubt that she could pull it off.

She had doubts, too. What she needed was her father's support and encouragement. She had neither. That hurt, so much so that it was a relief when he'd launched into a litany of complaints regarding the Brooklyn walkup his Realtor showed them. It was much too small, Oscar claimed. Never mind that it was ten times larger than Ella's current apartment and had half a dozen windows, a couple of which offered a decent view of a nearby park.

Its furnishings were subpar and showed signs of wear, Oscar lamented. Okay, so the table wasn't a Duncan Phyfe, but it was an actual table. And the queen-size bed he'd turned up his nose at had her lumpy futon beat all to hell.

In the end, Oscar told her he'd lost his appetite and would have to take a rain check on dinner. They'd parted ways outside the building he'd deemed to be in a slum. The Realtor left in his minivan after promising to be in touch soon. Oscar? He'd called for a car to take him back to Long Island. God only knew how he could afford it. Ella, meanwhile, had taken the subway to Lower Manhattan and hoofed the final three blocks home in sweltering heat. Her feet were still angry with her, which was why she was wearing ballet flats today.

She recapped the peanut butter and put both it and the chocolate syrup away. Where she'd learned to improvise and lower her expectations to match her reality, her father was determined to continue indulging his champagne taste on a budget that allowed for beer, and the cheap domestic variety, at that.

Ella sighed again. Then, pushing away thoughts of her father, she got to work. On the morning's agenda? Hand-delivering the invitations for Chase's dinner party and a lunch meeting with the manager of The Colton. The bonus? The samples she planned to taste would double as her lunch. It paid to be inventive.

Two hours later, all of the invitations had been delivered except one: Elliot's. Of course, he already knew the date and place, since they'd discussed it in his office only the day before, but she'd gone ahead and filled one out for him. Attention to detail. That was going to be one of the hallmarks of her new business. Now she stood in the lobby of Trumbull Toys debating the wisdom of boarding the elevator and possibly running into Chase.

Ella had no regrets about yesterday—except that it had had to end. She wasn't a shy virgin and wouldn't feel awkward seeing him today. But she didn't want to make it seem as if she was stalking him simply because they'd spent a memorable few hours in the sack.

"I'm a professional," she muttered aloud and punched the up button. "I'm here for a legitimate reason."

"And what reason might that be?"

She turned to find Owen behind her.

"Delivering an invitation to your uncle."

"For Chase's little party?"

She nodded, not caring for the derisive tone, even if she now understood the reason behind it.

"I can give it to him if you'd like. I don't mind playing your delivery boy."

He held out his hand, tracing a finger over her cheek. This went beyond flirting. Ella stepped away.

"Thanks, but I need to see Elliot anyway."

Owen shrugged. The elevator arrived and they boarded. After it started its ascent, Ella fixed her gaze on the digital display above the door, watching the number change as they passed each floor.

They were closing in on nine when Owen asked, "So, what's on the agenda for Chase's soiree? I'm guessing boring conversation, old-fashioned cocktails and bland food. My cousin doesn't do spicy."

Ella didn't care for his belittling remarks. Or his not-so-veiled swipe at his cousin's manhood. Chase might not be the sort to advertise the party to be found in his pants, but that didn't mean it wasn't there. As she'd discovered firsthand.

"Could have fooled me," she murmured before she could think better of it.

From the corner of her eye, she caught Owen's surprised look. "What's that supposed to mean?"

"Nothing."

But he wasn't put off. "Don't tell me—you and Chase?"

Ella had to work to keep a smile from turning up the corners of her mouth. She'd dived headfirst into the deep end of the still water that was Chase Trumbull and had enjoyed doing the backstroke.

Owen snorted before laughing outright. His mirth left her uneasy.

"Diddling with the hired help," he drawled. "I didn't know my cousin had it in him. He's been such a stickler for rules in the workplace since he came on board at Trumbull. Sucked the fun right out of the place."

Owen's diddling comment was intended to get a rise out of her. Ella knew that. But she took the bait anyway and offered a slow wink when she told him, "Chase and I diddled off the clock and away from the workplace. No rules were broken."

Owen's eyes went flat, even as he grinned. "If you want to try out the company's first string, let me know. I'm happy to oblige."

When the doors opened a moment later, she was eager to step out of the elevator and bid Owen goodbye. Chase's door was ajar, but he wasn't at his desk. Elliot's door was closed. Ella shot a smile in the direction of the dourly dressed trio seated behind the reception desk. To her surprise, the foosball table she remembered from the documentary was back.

"I have an invitation to deliver to Elliot, as well as some suggestions for the entertainment for his party," she added last minute. He hadn't actually asked for any during yesterday's meeting, but they gave her a bona fide reason beyond the invitation to be here. "Is he in?"

"Yes, but he's busy at the moment. You can give everything to me," the woman who'd given her the guest list for the wake offered.

That posed a problem, since the list Ella had concocted was only in her head. She handed over the invitation and said, "I'll call him later to discuss my suggestions. Or shoot him an email."

She was crossing to the elevator when Chase came out of Elliot's office and called her name.

His smile was warm, his gaze hot.

"Here to see me?" he asked.

"Elliot actually. I was just dropping off his invitation to your party." She smiled smugly. "All of them have been delivered."

"You've had a busy morning."

She nodded, suddenly tongue-tied when she recalled how "busy" they'd been the day before. She glanced away and her gaze landed on the foosball table.

She pointed to it. "I like the new addition."

"It's actually old. I had it brought out of storage this morning."

"You did?"

"Someone mentioned something about happy cows..." He shrugged. "I'm thinking of having monthly tournaments."

"You're just full of surprises." And wasn't that the truth? He was wearing a tie, perfectly knotted, but figuratively, at least, he'd loosened it.

"I've ordered a few more that will go in the cafeteria. Which reminds me, do you have plans for lunch?"

"Actually, I do. I'm heading over to The Colton. The manager is having samples made up of the menu items I requested for your dinner. I get to try them."

"Want some company?" he asked.

How to play this, Ella wondered. She opted to be casual. "It's your party."

"Is that a yes?"

"It's not a no."

He frowned. "And that's not an answer."

Casual was getting complicated. She decided to be blunt. "I don't want you to feel obligated, because, well…" She lowered her voice. "Because of yesterday."

His lips twitched with an almost smile. "That's thoughtful, but unnecessary. I don't feel…obligated."

But he did feel something and based on the way his gaze was lingering on her mouth, Ella had a good idea what it might be. Too bad they were heading to a public place or a replay of the previous day would be inevitable. She shivered just thinking about it.

"I can hang out for a few minutes if you need to do something before we leave. Or you can meet me at the restaurant." That was casual *and* uncomplicated. She gave herself a mental high-five.

"I have nothing pressing right now. We can go."

Unfortunately, Owen stepped out of his office just then.

"Where are you off to, Chase?" He smirked before adding, "As if I need to ask."

"Ella and I have an appointment with the manager of The Colton. We're sampling the menu for my dinner party."

"Sampling." He nodded. "A nice word for a nooner."

Chase's gaze turned hard as steel and he took a menacing step toward Owen. Ella headed off what she decided would be an ugly exchange by grabbing his arm.

With an overly bright smile, she said, "Let's go. I don't want to be late."

"I'll apologize for my cousin," Chase said when they were in the elevator heading to the lobby.

"Don't. If anyone should be apologizing, it's me." Ella took a deep breath and admitted, "It was thanks to my big mouth that he put two and two together."

Far from being angry, Chase appeared amused. "You didn't strike me as the sort to kiss and tell."

"Generally speaking, I'm not. It's just that Owen made a comment about you being boring and not liking anything spicy, and I..." Ella wrinkled her nose and decided to leave it at that.

Chase filled in the blank for her. "You came to my defense."

"It seemed like a good idea at the time. You're not mad?"

"More like flattered that you felt compelled to disabuse him of the notion. Thank you."

Chase stepped closer, bringing the crisp scent of his aftershave with him.

"Well, he was wrong," she murmured and closed the distance. Ella rested the palms of her hands on his chest and inhaled deeply. "I love the way you smell."

His scent had lingered on her body after they'd parted ways the previous day. It had been with a great deal of regret that she'd washed it away when she'd showered last night.

"I'm pretty partial to the way you smell, too."

He dipped his head, kissed her lips. Fantasies involving hitting the emergency stop button bubbled in Ella's brain. But that one kiss was all they had time for before the doors opened at the lobby.

CHAPTER NINE

"ARE YOU SURE you don't need me to go with you and help set up?" Sandra asked as they sat on the futon in Ella's apartment.

Ella was triple-checking her notes. Sandra was filing her nails. Ella wasn't fooled. Her friend didn't want to lend a hand as much as she wanted a good look at Chase. Ella shook her head.

"It's a dinner party for eight people. If I can't handle this on my own, there's absolutely no hope for me in the business."

"You can handle it." Sandra stopped filing. "You seem to really like this job."

"I do." Ella looked up from her notes and grinned. "I mean, what's not to like about parties, right?"

"Yes, but planning them isn't the same as attending them. It can't be all fun and games."

"No." A lot of tedium was involved, as Ella was discovering. She'd touched base twice already with The Colton about the food, and had headed off a crisis over the centerpiece when the florist called earlier that morning to say the shipment of sky-blue hydrangeas had not arrived. Plan B involved pale green hydrangeas, which would still complement the tablescape Ella had in mind. "You know, I think I may be good at this."

"Better than you are at identifying the next fashion trend?" Sandra asked.

"Maybe."

Ella shrugged. Her intuition regarding which colors, cuts and textures were going to be hot would have made her a good buyer, or so one of her professors at NYU had claimed. But she discovered that she used some of that same intuition planning a party. Even food could be fashionable, and some trends were overdone in her opinion.

Was party-planning what she was meant to do with her life? She wasn't sure, regardless of what Madame Maroushka thought. But Ella did know that for the first time in a long time she had money in the bank, was current on her rent and she was enjoying herself.

Chase came to mind, an image of the two of them sweaty and sated and already gearing up for another go-round. He wasn't the only reason she was enjoying herself, but Ella wouldn't discount his effect on her current mood.

Sandra sighed. "I envy you, El."

The admission caught Ella by surprise.

The women had been friends since their freshman year at an exclusive all-girl prep school, the tuition for which rivaled some of the best universities in the country. Sandra still lived in one of Manhattan's most exclusive ZIP codes. She was dating a man who adored her, a decent guy who, by all indications, wanted to marry her, and who easily could afford to keep Sandra in the lifestyle to which she was accustomed. Her family was well regarded in the community. Her mother was on a first-name basis with the mayor. As for her father, he'd never been the punch line for a late-night comedian's joke. She'd never been put on the stand in a courtroom or grilled by strangers about her father's business dealings. Nor had she been chased by tabloid reporters eager for a quote. She didn't have a stepmother who went around badmouthing her or a stepsister who just plain hated her and loved making her life miserable.

Ella stopped what she was doing and asked in bewilderment, "How can you possibly envy me?"

"You're so Zen about everything. And, once you set your mind to something, you never waver. You go after it. No hesitation."

"I don't have a choice," Ella pointed out.

Sandra shrugged. "Still, you know who you are."

Ella wouldn't claim to have her life figured out. If she had, she wouldn't have consulted Madame Maroushka. But her friend was right. Ella did know who she was. "That's because I'm the same person I've always been."

"Exactly." Sandra put the emery board aside and began fiddling with an earring, a sure sign that she was anxious about something. "Your circumstances changed. Drastically. But you, you stayed the same, El."

"You stayed the same, too. A lot of people stopped calling me or they stopped taking my calls after my dad was accused of insider trading. And then when the lawsuits started…" Ella shook her head to clear it of the painful memories. "You were never one of those people, though. You stuck by me. You stayed true."

"BFFs through thick and thin," Sandra replied, letting go of the silver hoop that dangled from her earlobe to stick out her hand.

They linked little fingers and giggled like the schoolgirls they'd been the first time they'd executed a pinky oath. Then Sandra sobered.

"I can't stop wondering if I'd be as resilient as you've been if our situations were reversed."

"Oh, you would. You totally would," Ella assured her, although she hoped Sandra never had to find out.

Sandra nodded, but then to Ella's surprise, the young

woman covered her face with her hands and wailed, "I invited Bernadette to my family's barbecue."

"You wh—!" Ella moderated her tone and asked, "When did this happen? How?"

Sandra lowered her hands. "Yesterday. Cole and I were out at Belmont Park watching Deuce's Pride race. While we were there we ran into Bradley." No surprise that. Bradley entertained illusions of becoming a breeder. Sandra's boyfriend, meanwhile, owned several horses, which he stabled near the storied track. "Anyway, Cole and Bradley had their heads together about horses. The next thing I knew, Cole was saying, 'We'll talk more at the barbecue.' You know guys. He just assumed Bradley was on the guest list even though he hasn't been welcome at my house since he broke off things with you."

"And so you invited Bernadette?"

"Not intentionally. But when Bradley asked what time *they* should arrive, meaning he and Bernadette, I didn't tell him to go to hell. Feel free to hate me, because I said, three o'clock. God! I am the worst friend ever!" Sandra wailed again.

"It's not your fault," Ella murmured, even as her heart sank. She'd been looking forward to going, not only because she always had a good time, but to pick Mrs. Chesterfield's brain about the mechanics behind organizing such a large bash. The guest list routinely topped two hundred. Now? She would have to worry about running into her ex and Bernadette.

Still, to Sandra, Ella said, "Your family's barbecue is huge. I shouldn't have a hard time avoiding them."

"I have a better idea," Sandra said. "Bring a date. Bring Chase."

This wasn't the first time her friend had made the suggestion, but Ella declined once again, shaking her head for emphasis.

"Why not?"

"I've already told you. Chase and I aren't a couple."

"You're just sleeping together?" Sandra arched one eyebrow. "That doesn't sound like you."

No, it didn't. As a rule, Ella wasn't casual about sex, but she was trying to be with Chase. He hadn't said anything about the future, but she knew he had a home in Los Angeles, a job there he would be returning to eventually.

"I'm not saying I don't like him." And wasn't that an understatement? The more Ella got to know Chase the more reasons she found to fall for him. "But he's not my boyfriend."

"Ella?"

"He's not. We haven't even been out on a proper date." Sampling menu items at The Colton didn't count. Nor did the incredible sex they'd had twice since then.

"All right. But you could still bring him to the barbecue, make Bradley jealous."

"Please. Bradley is over me."

"Okay, make Bernadette green with envy then. Chase is a better catch than Bradley any day."

"Point taken."

More to get Sandra off her back than because Ella was seriously considering asking Chase, she promised not to rule out the possibility.

Chase tugged at the knot in his tie as he waited for Ella to arrive. According to his doorman, who'd called a minute earlier, she'd been let into the private elevator and was on her way up. When the doors slid open, all Chase saw were flowers and a skimpy skirt that revealed a pair of long and shapely legs. His mouth went slack, even as other parts of his body grew tight. And that was before she peeked from behind the flower arrangement and glossy pink lips curved with a moan-inducing smile.

"What do you think?" she asked.

"Gorgeous."

Ella nodded at the flowers as she stepped off the elevator. "They are, aren't they? The florist was worried when the original color I ordered wasn't available, but I think I like these better actually."

He'd been talking about the woman, not the blooms, but he didn't correct Ella.

"Let me have those." He took the flowers from her hands. "I assume they go on the table."

"So smart," she teased as she followed him to the dining room. Once there, however, she instructed him to put them on the sideboard. "They're one of the final touches to my tablescape."

"Your what?"

"Tablescape." Ella set a stuffed backpack-style purse on one of the chairs. "It's…never mind," she finished on a chuckle. Then, "Don't you look…formal."

"Too much?" he asked.

It wasn't like him to worry over wardrobe choices, much less rethink them, but he was now.

"It depends on the tone you want to set for the dinner party and what your guests will be wearing. The goal of a good host is to ensure that his guests are as at ease in his home as they are in their own." She laughed. "I read that online."

She was taking her new career very seriously, which was good considering all that was at stake for his uncle. Through a great deal of persuasion behind the scenes, Chase had been able to get the board to hold off on the vote to oust Elliot. He hoped to use the time to expose the leak and talk his uncle into getting the medical help he needed. The party, however, loomed overhead like an ominous dark cloud. The seasoned planner he'd hired to shadow Ella would ensure all of the bases were covered. Chase wouldn't feel guilty about that. He couldn't.

"My guests probably won't be wearing ties," he admitted.

The men would be in jackets, but they would leave off the neckwear. Chase reached up to remove his, keeping his gaze on Ella. Her eyes were glued to the knot just below his Adam's apple. Was she remembering the last time they'd been in this room and he'd removed his tie? He certainly was.

Then her gaze cut away and she rubbed her hands together. "So, you said you had white linens and place settings for eight."

She was eager to begin. Chase was eager, too, but it had nothing to do with setting a table and preparing for guests, which weren't due to arrive for another three hours.

Three hours. That left plenty of time for…

"Linens, Chase." Her smile, more so than her words, told him she knew exactly where his mind had wandered. "And I'm not talking about bed sheets."

"We have three hours," he pointed out.

"Exactly. And as much as I wouldn't mind a repeat of the other day, I need to use the time to get ready." She swallowed, nibbled her lower lip. "This is important."

Of course it was important. It was Ella's first party as a planner. In a small—very small—way, it was her dress rehearsal for Elliot's bash. So, with a sigh, Chase reeled in his libido and gave her arm a reassuring squeeze.

"It's going to be perfect."

"It better be. If I can't manage a party this size…"

For the first time since he'd known her, Ella appeared truly distressed, and Chase realized that while he'd been focused on how much was at stake for his uncle, he'd forgotten how much Ella had on the line. He told his conscience he was doing her a favor by providing backup, albeit covertly.

"It's natural to be nervous."

"I guess so."

"Linens," he said resolutely.

Chase had asked Elliot's butler to go through his mother's things, which were stored in the estate's attic, and send over what he needed. Several boxes had been delivered the previous day, but Chase hadn't opened them yet. Luckily, Dermott had labeled them.

Chase opened the flaps on the one marked LINENS and pulled out an ivory table cloth and matching napkins that hadn't seen the light of day in more than two decades.

"Nice," Ella murmured, running her fingers over the fabric. "Irish linen with hand-tatted lace."

"If you say so."

"It's very elegant. The perfect backdrop." She unfolded one of the napkins. "It looks like everything will need to be pressed." She glanced over at him. "Go turn on your iron."

"My iron?" He blinked.

"You do own one, right?"

"Ella, I send out everything that needs to be pressed."

"I should have realized…" She closed her eyes briefly before her expression brightened. "You know what? I've got it covered."

She grabbed the cell phone from her purse and punched in a number.

"Sandra? It's Ella," she said when the other person answered. "It looks like I need your help after all."

While they waited for her friend to ride to the rescue with Ella's iron, Chase helped Ella unpack the dishes from another box.

"Your mother had great taste," Ella remarked, lifting a bone china plate edged in gold from its protective wrapping.

Chase vaguely recalled seeing it one Thanksgiving. He'd

been six or seven years old at the time, and the reason the occasion stuck in his head was because he'd accidentally broken a matching dessert plate, and she'd been livid.

"Great taste," he agreed with a nod. "It was maternal instincts she lacked."

How else to explain how the woman could leave her child behind without a backward glance?

He waited for Ella's apology. Chase didn't share his story often, but whenever he had this was where women told him how sorry they were. Not Ella.

She said, "That sucks."

Her candor had him snorting in surprise. "Yeah. It does."

"My mom was really good at mothering. She considered it her career. She could have had a job. She had a business degree and had worked in a brokerage firm before she met and married my dad. But she chose to stay at home, which of course, she could afford to do. Still, a lot of her friends who stayed home after having kids hired nannies."

"I had a nanny," Chase said.

"My mom said she didn't want anyone else raising her child."

"She sounds wonderful."

"She was." Ella tipped her head to one side on a sigh. "I always thought it was ironic that even though she didn't want anyone else raising her child, that was what wound up happening anyway."

In lieu of offering condolences, which he doubted she wanted and which were sure to turn the mood maudlin, Chase repeated her phrase.

"That sucks."

"Big time." Ella's tone was wistful when she asked, "Do you ever wonder what your life would have been like if your mom had stuck around after your dad died?"

"I used to. For several months after I moved into Uncle Elliot's house, I laid awake at night listening for the sound of her heels on the hardwood in the hallway. I was sure she'd come back for me." Chase swallowed after making the admission. What was it about Ella that made it so easy to share secrets that he'd kept from everyone else? "What about you? Do you ever wonder how things might be if your mom were alive?"

She nodded. "At first, I pretended my mom was just on an extended vacation. About the year mark, I started telling people that she'd been captured by pirates." Her laughter was dry but not without humor. "My mom would have loved that. Not actually being captured by pirates, but my imaginative explanation."

"She sounds like a lot of fun." And, from what Chase could tell, the apple hadn't fallen far from the tree.

Ella nodded. "When my dad started to date again, that's when I finally accepted that she was gone."

Chase recalled what she had told him when they'd run into Camilla at The Colton. Ella had wanted a mother, but Camilla hadn't been interested in being one to her.

"I think you must have a lot of your mom in you."

"Thanks." Those quirky dimples flashed with her smile. "For as much as my life would have been different if my mother were still around, I don't think I would be. My friend Sandra and I were just talking about that. I haven't changed."

Chase had to agree. They may not have known one another for long, but it was apparent that Ella's cup was always half-full. He pulled a crystal wine goblet from the box in front of him. Had he always viewed his half-empty or had his pessimism begun after his father's death and his mother's desertion?

Ella's gasp drew his attention. He glanced over to see her holding up a spoon and frowning. The filigree detail on the utensil's handle was hard to make out because of the tarnish.

"I don't suppose you have any silver polish?" she said.

"Sure. It's right next to my iron."

"That's what I was afraid of." She reached for her cell phone again.

By the time the doorman announced her friend's arrival an hour later, Ella already had washed the plates, bowls, serving pieces and glasses they would need, and had cleared off the sideboard to make room for an ice bucket and all of the fixings for a couple of trendy cocktails, whose recipes she'd gone over with him.

She'd moved the vase and a pair of pewter candlesticks that usually graced his dining room table and brought in from the living room a couple of dust-catching orb-shaped knickknacks, all of which had come with the furnished penthouse. Even though he saw them every day, she somehow made them seem new. It was as if they were intended to be showcased together on the sideboard.

It was interesting to watch her work, to watch the same dimples that winked with her smile dent her cheeks now when, lost in thought, she nibbled her lower lip.

Just as he had shed his suit coat and rolled up the sleeves of his oxford shirt, Ella had long ago kicked off a pair of dangerously high heels and lost the loose-knit turquoise sweater that she'd layered over a plain white tank top. Barefoot and wearing only the tank and a denim miniskirt, she didn't exactly look professional, not how he had come to define it anyway. But he couldn't argue with her results.

Nor could he argue with the fact that he found her concentration a huge turn-on. Unfortunately, they no longer were alone.

"Sandra! Thank God!" Ella cried, as soon as the other woman walked into the penthouse. "Do you have everything I asked you to bring?"

"Iron from your apartment and silver polish from the store. Check."

The dark-haired woman directed her response to Ella, but her gaze was on Chase, sizing him up. Her smile told him he'd passed muster.

"This is Chase. Chase, this is my best friend and your savior, Sandra."

"It's nice to meet you. And thanks." He took the bag from her arms.

"It's nice to meet you, too. And you're welcome."

"Um, you don't need to stick around," Ella said when Sandra set her purse on the couch. "I have everything under control now."

"Oh, I don't doubt that," her friend replied. But instead of saying goodbye, Sandra turned to Chase and asked, "Has Ella mentioned my family's barbecue?"

"Sandra!" Ella's cheeks had turned fuchsia.

Curious and a little amused, Chase played along. "Barbecue? No. She hasn't."

"It's an annual thing that my parents host to raise money for diabetes research."

"Sandra's brother was diagnosed as a child," Ella supplied. The flush was fading from her face, but her eyes were shooting daggers at her friend.

"That's too bad," Chase replied. "I had a friend in school who had Type I. Insulin shots every day and one very close call when his sugar got out of whack. It was miserable."

"Yes. Tony is an adult now, but my parents say they will keep having their barbecue to raise funds until a cure is found. They've raised several million dollars so far."

"Wow. That's impressive. As is their dedication."

Sandra smiled. "This year's barbecue is the weekend after next."

Chase had a pretty good idea where this conversation was heading, but from Ella's expression he wasn't sure how she felt about it.

"The food is excellent and my parents always have first-rate entertainment. Isn't that right, Ella?"

"First-rate," she mumbled, looking as if she could kill her friend.

"Ella wasn't planning parties yet or I'm sure my parents would have hired her. Anyway, if you're not busy, you're welcome to stop by. It kicks off around three and goes till whenever. Silent auction winners are announced at eight, and the live auction starts at six." Sandra smiled innocently before adding, "You can come with Ella."

Chase offered a noncommittal nod since it didn't appear Ella had planned to invite him.

Her friend left not long after that, and Ella got down to business ironing the tablecloth and napkins. She shooed him away when he offered to help.

"You hired me to do this," she reminded him, pointing the business end of the iron at him.

Palms up, he backed away. Not long after that, the door-man called to announce the delivery of the food.

"Oh, my God! It's early!" Ella exclaimed with a glance at the wall clock. "Your guests aren't going to be here for another hour and a half."

"I'll handle this."

But once again, she refused. "No. Go do whatever it is you do when you're getting ready to entertain."

Expression grim, she grabbed her cell phone and called the restaurant. Chase pitied whoever had the misfortune of answering.

Ella could have waited till morning to call Chase and learn how the evening turned out. But with excitement and nerves waging a tug-of-war in the pit of her stomach, she gave in and punched in his number just after eleven o'clock.

He answered on the third ring.

"I was wondering when you were going to call," he said.

"Am I that predictable?"

"Hardly. Actually, I hoped you would stop in for a late-night snack. I have some of those stuffed portobello mushrooms left."

The intimate timbre of his tone had gooseflesh prickling Ella's arms. She had a pretty good idea what kind of snack Chase had in mind and it had nothing to do with leftovers. But sex wasn't the reason, or at least it wasn't the only reason, for her call.

"Do you have a lot of food still?"

She hoped not, but if he did, it wouldn't be because the meat had dried out or gone cold. Ella had verbally chewed out the manager at The Colton for sending everything over early, and she'd promptly sent it back with the delivery man with instructions that the order be made from scratch and arrive at the agreed-upon time.

Low laughter greeted her question. "You have a one-track mind."

"I could say the same about you."

He chuckled a second time. "The food got rave reviews from everyone. Almost all of the appetizers went. The stuffed mushrooms were a hit, just as you predicted, but I put a couple aside for you."

"Thoughtful."

"It gets better. I also saved you a slice of strawberry cheesecake."

Her mouth watered. "You're a saint."

"Given what I'm picturing us doing after you eat it, calling me a saint is a bit of a stretch."

Grinning, she asked, "What about the beef tips?"

"There were enough left for one meal. I sent them home with Uncle Elliot."

"Did he enjoy himself?"

"Yes."

Even in that one syllable, she heard concern. "Chase?"

"He arrived late, said he'd mixed up the date even though I spoke to him earlier in the day to remind him. Then, throughout the meal, he seemed…scattered."

"Have you had any luck on getting him to the doctor? He needs to be seen by a specialist, whether he wants to go or not."

"I know." Chase sighed. "I called my physician and asked for a referral. He gave me the name of one of the most respected neurologists in the field. I mentioned it to Elliot. He doesn't see the need. He said he's fine."

"He's probably just scared. I'd be if suddenly I couldn't remember simple things."

"I don't know what else to do," Chase admitted.

They talked a little longer, touching on inconsequential topics. While they spoke, she pulled the futon flat. The thunking sound it made wasn't overly loud, but Chase must have heard it.

"What was that?"

"The futon. I'm getting ready for bed."

They both were silent for several seconds. Then he said, "You're probably tired."

"You'd think so. In fact, I'm wide awake, thanks to nerves and excitement. My first party was a success."

"That was never in doubt."

"Thanks for that."

"For what?"

"Having faith in me. You don't know what that means."

"Ella…I…I do have faith in you." His emphatic tone seemed out of place. But then he was saying, "I should let you go."

"Yeah. It's late," she agreed, albeit disappointed.

A few seconds of silence ticked by during which she could hear Chase breathing. His labored breaths matched her own.

"Ella?" he said at last.

"Uh-huh?"

"It's not *that* late."

Her heart knocked out an extra couple of beats. "What do you have in mind?"

She'd been thinking phone sex. But she liked his idea much better, when he replied, "I'll tell you when I get there."

CHAPTER TEN

WITH CHASE'S PARTY out of the way—and by all accounts a success—Ella began to focus in earnest on Elliot's wake. The older man had signed off on the invitations. Ella was especially pleased with her design: white ink on black cardstock that was layered over another piece of white cardstock, both of which were held together with a quarter-inch-wide piece of grosgrain ribbon. Elegant, sedate, they set the tone.

Ella had addressed and mailed all of them a week earlier. Already a few dozen of the 692 guests had confirmed their attendance.

Nearly seven hundred guests! OMG!

With just six weeks left to plan it, she already had spent more than a few sleepless nights thinking about the logistics involved.

Before the invitations had gone out, she'd tried to talk Elliot into having the wake in the city. Several hotels had banquet facilities that could accommodate such a large party, with the added bonus of providing valet parking, catering, bar services and a wait staff. But he'd been adamant about hosting it on his estate. That meant she had to hire people to perform all of those services.

Even if she got lucky and the weather was gorgeous on the day of the event, Ella needed to have places for everyone to sit, to eat and facilities for them to use when nature called. Chase had reminded her of that, although she'd already figured it out for herself. He was full of suggestions, and a surprisingly good sounding board. Despite the unorthodox way she'd launched her business and the job he'd given her out of pity, he took her seriously. He believed in her. Talk about a powerful aphrodisiac. But then, what was going on between them went beyond sex. At least it did for her.

California.

Ella had made it her buzz word. Every time she found herself falling for him, she said it as a reminder that eventually he would return to his home on the West Coast.

She'd been repeating those four syllables a lot lately.

On the agenda for this day was visiting Elliot's estate so she could draft a layout and determine where everything would be set up.

She had blocked off what remained of the morning for their meeting, as well as a couple of hours in the early afternoon if need be. But she wanted to wrap up by two o'clock. Sandra's family barbecue started at three. To save herself time, as well as a trip back into the city, Ella had a garment bag with the outfit she was going to wear. And, since Sandra's mother had insisted Ella stay the remainder of the weekend, an overnight bag was packed and sitting near the door.

Elliot had called the day before to say he would be sending a car to fetch her. As Ella waited, she consulted her notes, which already had grown from a few paragraphs to a few dozen pages, and were now organized alphabetically and cross-referenced by potential vendors and typed into her handy new tablet—a gift from Chase.

Elliot may have told her that cost was no object, but Ella was determined to get the best price and value for the money she spent. That meant getting estimates. And getting estimates took time, more time than Ella felt she had to spare. But it couldn't be helped.

When the buzzer sounded—the super had repaired the intercom system at Chase's insistence—she pressed the intercom and said, "I'll be right down."

She didn't wait for a reply. Instead, she stuffed the tablet into her purse, slung it and the overnight bag over one shoulder, snagged the garment bag and headed down.

She was out of breath by the time she reached the lobby. The sight that greeted her did little to improve her lung capacity. Chase was waiting outside. He was dressed in a pair of khaki pants and a white button-down shirt whose sleeves he'd rolled halfway up his forearms. It was as casual as she'd ever seen him, and she had to say, she liked the look, especially since his expression was as relaxed as his attire.

She grinned as she opened the door. "I didn't realize you were the one who had buzzed, or I would have let you in rather than racing down here with all my stuff."

"So I gather. Taking a trip?" He took the garment bag from her hands as he spoke and then transferred the strap of the overnight bag to his shoulder.

"Not a trip. I have…a thing tonight," she finished.

Ella had debated formally extending to Chase the invitation Sandra had tossed out before his dinner party. The two of them had spent a lot of time together since then, either at his penthouse or in her tiny efficiency. He didn't mind coming to her less-than-luxurious place.

He'd done so after his dinner party, arriving at midnight with the slice of cheesecake he'd saved for her in hand and a gleam in his eye that had turbo-charged her hormones. They'd made fast work of stripping each other down to bare skin, after which they put her futon to good use. An hour shy of dawn, they shared the dessert before finally falling asleep.

To Ella's disappointment, she'd awoken alone just after nine o'clock. A note was on the pillow that Chase had used.

I didn't want to wake you, but I had to go. I'll call you later. —C

C for Chase.

C for casual.

C for California.

Inviting him to attend Sandra's party as her date seemed to cross a line that both of them had drawn, even if neither of them had said so aloud. They were an item, but they weren't exactly a couple. The *C* didn't stand for that.

"Your friend's barbecue," he said now.

Hmm, so he had remembered.

She nodded and added, "I'm spending the night at Sandra's parents' place. But before then, I have a meeting with your uncle." She glanced up the block, scanned the handful of cars, taxicabs and delivery trucks. "Elliot said he would send a car for me. When you buzzed, I thought you were the driver."

"I am." Half of his mouth quirked up as he deposited her garment bag and small carry-on in the trunk of his car. "When I heard he was sending someone for you, I volunteered."

Ella grinned in full. "How thoughtful."

"You only say that because you can't read my mind," he replied, his gaze turning intimate.

She laughed before rising on tiptoe to brush her lips against his. As she started to ease away, however, Chase hauled her back for a proper, curl-your-toes kiss.

"Did you have to stop?" she murmured breathlessly when he drew back.

"Unfortunately. We don't have time for anything else. My uncle is expecting you and, as you mentioned, you have plans yourself later on."

Oh, this was awkward, Ella decided, as fog from the kiss cleared from her brain.

"Um, about that. Elliot had offered to have his driver take me over to Sandra's parents' house in the Hamptons since it's not that far from his estate."

"I know. I will."

"You don't mind?"

"Not at all."

He opened the passenger door and Ella got in. She only had a few seconds to make up her mind as she watched him jog around the hood of the car to his door.

When he opened it, she asked, "Do you want to come with me?"

"To the barbecue?"

"Yes."

Chase slid the key in the ignition and started the car. Cool air poured from the vents, which was a good thing given the heat outside. It didn't help that Ella was in the proverbial hot seat thanks to her friend's big mouth.

"Look, Ella, you don't have to feel obligated to invite me just because I've agreed to drive you there."

"I don't. I want you to come."

She said it quickly, perhaps a little too quickly, she decided, when Chase frowned.

"Ella—"

She lifted her shoulders. "If you don't want to go with me, I understand how things are."

Even though he had just eased his car into traffic, he hit the brake and shifted back into Park. Behind them, horns blared. He unrolled his window to put his hand out and wave them around. Then he gave Ella his full attention.

"What is it you think you understand?"

"Well, just that we aren't *that* kind of couple."

"That makes things clear as mud," he grumbled. "What kind of couple do you think we are?"

The casual kind. The kind that sleeps together. Even though she didn't say the words aloud, they left a sour taste in her mouth.

"We're not the kind of couple that spends time with family and close friends. Well, my family and close friends," she clarified, since she already had spent plenty of time with Chase's uncle and de facto father and would do so again today.

He appeared ready to argue. His brow knitted and his mouth opened. But he clamped it shut, shifted the car into gear once again, and without another word, merged into traffic.

Was he mad?

If she had to pin an emotion to his current mood, perplexed would fit. Well, that made two of them who were confused. Other than awkward small talk, the drive to El-liot's was accomplished in silence.

Elliot's Long Island estate was much as Ella had expected it to be. That is to say, ginormous. And, much like his office in the city, it was a child's fantasy brought to life with a full-size Ferris wheel and a go-cart track that snaked around a huge inground swimming pool, over a bridge and under a waterfall.

"This is awesome," she whispered. Even if it was going to complicate her layout plans significantly.

Chase parked in the circular drive, the centerpiece of which was a fountain where a trio of life-size elephant sculptures spouted water from their upturned trunks.

"*Absurd* is the word a lot of people use." But his expression bordered on fondness. To her relief, the awkwardness from earlier appeared to have dissipated. "Wait till you meet Dermott. You'll understand."

She did.

When the door opened, a man of about seventy stood in the foyer wearing unrelieved black. The color was sedate.

The style? Avant-garde would have been putting it mildly. A vest and genie pants. Yet the older man, chin raised in such a way that he appeared to be looking down his nose, carried it off with a definite air of dignity.

Chase didn't smile, but his expression told her he wanted to. "Hello, Dermott. I see you haven't talked Elliot into a new uniform yet."

"Not yet, sir. No. But hope springs eternal. This must be Miss Sanborn," the butler added then, a hint of British in his speech.

"It is."

"It's nice to meet you," she said.

"The same. Your uncle is expecting you both. I believe you will find him in the media room."

"How is he?" Chase asked quietly.

Dermott glanced at Ella. "It's as we discussed on the telephone yesterday."

From Chase's expression, whatever the two of them had discussed was not good.

"I see."

"May I bring you something to drink?" Dermott asked before they could brush past him. "Lunch won't be served for another half an hour."

Chase glanced at Ella. "A glass of water would be great, with a slice of lemon if you've got it," she said

Dermott nodded. "And you, Master Chase?"

"The same, but bring me a couple of extra-strength aspirin instead of the lemon."

"Very good."

"Do you have a headache?" Ella asked as she followed Chase through the home.

"No. But I will."

Chase had predicted a headache. He should have predicted nausea, as well. His stomach started to churn as soon as they entered the media room. Elliot was dressed, but hadn't shaved and his hair made it appear as if he'd just rolled out of bed. It stuck out in random tufts on his head. He was seated in the last of six rows of high-backed leather chairs, munching on popcorn as he watched an animated movie.

He flashed a delighted grin when he saw them.

"Oh, good. You're right on time. Come and have a seat. The next episode is just about to start." He nodded to the screen. "No one makes cartoons today that can hold a candle to the classics put out by William Hanna and Joseph Barbera."

"Oh, my God! I know!" Ella took the seat next to Elliot and reached for some popcorn.

She and his uncle were a matched set. Or they would have been if Elliot's eccentricities were merely that. Chase was troubled by his uncle's disheveled appearance and that was before Elliot smiled at Ella and said, "I knew I liked you. Remind me again who you are."

Ella paused with a handful of popcorn midway to her mouth. Her tone was gentle, her eyes full of understanding, even as Elliot's had clouded with confusion.

"I'm Ella. I'm here about your wake."

"Oh, God! I'm dying?" Elliot's face crumpled.

She immediately dropped the popcorn and reached for his hand with both of hers. "No. You're fine. Perfectly fine, Elliot."

It was a lie, but one Chase was grateful for at the moment. Elliot was getting worse. Ella was right that he needed to be seen by a doctor. Even if the diagnosis was Alzheimer's, Elliot, Owen and Chase all needed to know exactly what they were dealing with, what could be done to help, and what the future held.

"Why am I having a wake then?" Elliot asked.

"It's not really a wake. You just wanted to call it that. It's actually just a big party."

"A party? I love parties. I've been known to throw some great ones, haven't I, Chase?"

"Yes," he managed around the lump in his throat.

"What are we celebrating?" Elliot wanted to know.

Ella didn't miss a beat. "Your long and storied career as the head of Trumbull Toys."

"I'm the guest of honor?"

The older man's expression brightened even as Chase's heart sank.

"Yes, you are," Ella told him.

She was still holding Elliot's hand. If she felt pity, she didn't show it. Instead, her smile was reassuring, so much so that Chase himself took comfort in it.

His heart squeezed. It was right then that he realized the danger he was in. He'd already fallen under Ella's spell. How could a man not? She was sexy, gorgeous, vivacious and fun. But what he was feeling right now went beyond being charmed by her exuberance or turned on by her looks.

"What's wrong, Chase?" his uncle asked. "You look like you might faint. Are you feeling well?"

Both Elliot and Ella were staring at him.

"I'm fine. Nothing's wrong."

Which wasn't exactly the same as everything being right. But could it be? He couldn't think straight. Hell, he was having trouble breathing. And that was before Elliot looked at him and asked, "What are you doing here?"

This time when Chase's heart squeezed it had nothing to do with soft emotions or the woman inspiring them.

"You were going to send a car for Ella. I offered to bring her out for your meeting instead."

Please remember. Please remember. Please remember. Chase begged silently. It was a small consolation when he got his wish, because part of him knew the day could be coming when Elliot would not recognize his own family.

"Yes. Of course you did. And I know why," Elliot added

slyly with a meaningful bob of his shaggy eyebrows. "She's a pretty thing. If I were a couple decades younger, I'd give you a run for your money, my boy."

Whereas a moment ago Elliot was totally clueless, suddenly he was aware of everything, including romantic undercurrents.

"Don't count yourself out, Elliot." Ella's mouth curved with a smile. "There's something to be said for a mature man."

"Oh, you'll have to watch yourself with this one, Chase. If you're not smart, she'll get away."

Actually, Chase would be the one to do the leaving, Ella thought. Maybe not soon, but eventually. He'd told her as much. His life was in California. And as much as he loved Elliot, he'd left Manhattan once before. He didn't want to come between his uncle and Owen. As he'd told her one night as they'd lain in bed after making love, he felt that his very presence here ensured their relationship remained strained. Ella was pretty sure no amount of distance would make a difference. For whatever reason, Elliot saw only his son's faults and his nephew's attributes. But she'd kept that to herself.

"Let's go into my study. I'm eager to see what sort of headway you've made on the arrangements, Ella."

The cartoons were forgotten. He was the Elliot of old when he hopped to his feet.

His study was twice as large as the office he kept in Manhattan. Its size wasn't the only difference. This space was as cluttered as the other was clean. There were no bows to whimsy here. It did not have a race track or a candy dispenser or an ice cream sundae station. From the articles she'd read, Ella knew this was where Elliot actually worked.

"It's a little…cluttered," Chase murmured. "I don't know

how he gets anything done in here, but I gave up trying to persuade him to organize years ago."

Ella glanced around at the piles of papers, drawings and prototypes that were in various stages of development. She wasn't as bothered by it as Chase apparently was.

"One man's clutter is another man's creative process," she said.

"I guess so," he said.

She gingerly picked her way over to the leather sofa, pushed a pile of papers to one side and sat down. She decided to get right down to business.

"Here's what I'm thinking for food. The invitation says dinner will be served at six, but we opted not to have the meal plated and brought to the table. And a single buffet line, or even a few—" as had been one of Chase's suggestions "—would be a nightmare.

"I want to do different buffet-style stations and have them set up around the grounds. The stations would serve different ethnic foods—Mexican at one, Chinese at another, and so on."

"How many?" Chase asked.

"Seven in all." She glanced at her notes and rattled off the other ethnicities she wanted to include. "Any of these can be substituted, of course."

"I like the idea. I like it a lot," Elliot told her.

She glanced at Chase, who was studying her thoughtfully. "I do, too."

She heaved a silent sigh of relief. "Terrific. As for dessert, I'd like to do the same. Not necessarily different ethnic sweets, but different stations. One can be for cake. Another to create ice cream sundaes. Pie."

"Crepes?" Elliot asked hopefully.

"It's your party," Ella replied on a grin, and made a note of it.

Twenty minutes later, when Dermott announced that

lunch was ready, they had a preliminary menu decided. Now they only had to determine where everything, including a photo booth, disc jockey and a dance floor, would be set up.

Elliot's wake at the estate he'd long ago dubbed The Big Top was indeed turning into a three-ring circus.

After a light lunch of smoked turkey, provolone cheese and baby arugula on flatbread, they headed outside. Ella had gotten a glimpse of the grounds on their drive in. But with her attention on the carnival rides, she hadn't appreciated the massive home's architecture, which included gambrel roofs, and beautiful stonework.

Nor was she prepared for the lush gardens that edged the perimeter of the grounds. Shrubs and topiaries groomed into the shapes of various circus animals roamed amid blooms that perfumed the air.

Ella was far from an expert in horticulture, so she asked Chase, "Do you know what plants will still be in bloom next month?"

"No, but Dermott will. Why?"

"We might want to in-fill with annuals to punch up the color if nothing is flowering."

He blinked, nodded. "Excellent idea."

The ground was nice and level, but it was going to be difficult to put up tents amid the rides. Farther from the house, Ella spied tennis courts.

She pointed to them. "I think we should put the tents there. What do you think?"

"It was going to be my suggestion, actually. The courts are due to be resurfaced soon anyway."

"Do you play, Ella?" Elliot asked.

"Nah." On a laugh, she admitted, "I never cared for the outfits. Same for golf."

"Chase plays."

He shrugged. "Not much these days, but when I was a kid I used to hit the ball around every now and then."

"Don't let Chase fool you. He was a natural," Elliot recounted fondly. "Owen, too. Even though my son was younger, he had a powerful backswing. They were evenly matched. In the summer when they were boys, I used to send them out with their rackets and a sleeve of balls. They'd be out there for hours."

"Our arms would be rubber afterward."

"It was a good way for the two of you to settle your grievances without coming to blows."

"Is that why you did it?" Chase asked, his tone infused with surprise.

"Of course. The two of you bickered so much otherwise," Elliot replied on a shrug. "Sometimes I thought you might kill each other. The rivalry, especially on Owen's end."

"I didn't think you noticed."

Elliot's eyes were clear, if focused on the past. "I noticed. If I have one regret it's that I contributed to it. I wanted Owen to look up to you, to be more like you. He's always been as smart as a whip, but he lacked your drive and discipline. He's always seen running Trumbull Toys as his birthright rather than a position that needs to be earned. I'm afraid he still does," Elliot said before changing the subject. "Where shall we set up those dessert stations you were telling me about, Ella?"

An hour later, her tour of the grounds almost done, they stood beside the heated, Olympic-size swimming pool.

"This is going to be the dance floor," Ella announced.

"Water ballet?"

Both sides of Chase's mouth crooked up in a smile. He did that a lot lately, smiled in full. She wondered if he realized it, if others realized it. Surely she couldn't be the only one to notice the change.

"Very funny. I'm going to have it covered. It's too large and its location too central to work around. A customized platform going over it will accomplish two things. First, it will make this usable space. And second, it will remove a safety hazard."

"Good thinking," Elliot said.

"The disc jockey can set up in front of the pool house," Chase said.

"Exactly my thought," she agreed.

By the time they returned inside, Ella had sketched out where everything would be, including the unsightly portable bathrooms, which she planned to tuck behind a temporary row of potted, six feet tall arborvitae that she would get from a nursery.

"It's been a very productive day," she said as they walked back through the house.

Elliot nodded. "Now we just have to decide on the food."

Both Chase and Ella stopped walking.

"We decided on the food, Uncle Elliot."

"Seven stations that will serve different kinds of ethnic specialties," Ella supplied.

Elliot scratched his head. "I don't recall. But last week was a blur. We were so busy with meetings. Weren't we, Chase?"

Neither Chase nor Ella pointed out that the decision had been made just that morning. Doing so seemed pointless, borderline cruel.

"You've been working a lot, Elliot. Those long hours can be hard on your health."

He waved off her concern. "I'm fit as a fiddle, thanks to all of those walks in the park. Nothing like a brisk walk to improve a man's vital functions."

"You should let your doctor determine that." She sent Chase a meaningful glance.

"I'm due for my yearly physical. I can make an appointment for you, as well," he offered.

Elliot became agitated. "No. No. You know how I feel about doctors."

"Uncle—"

That was as far as Chase got before Elliot changed the subject, "Can you stay for dinner? Dermott is making chicken wings in his trademark hot sauce."

"Sorry, Elliot. I can't."

"Ella has a barbecue," Chase said.

"Darn. You'd like those wings. Another time?"

"Definitely," she told him.

Elliot turned to Chase. "I suppose that means you can't stay either since you'll be going with her."

He would be driving her. As for attending the barbecue, they'd never settled that question.

Ella raised her brows in challenge. "Are you?"

Chase didn't hesitate. "I am."

CHAPTER ELEVEN

"He's getting worse," Ella said as soon as they left Elliot's house. "It's been just over a month since I met him and I see a marked decline in his short-term memory. He didn't even recall our conversation about the menu."

Beside her in the car, Chase nodded grim-faced, but he said nothing.

"He needs to be seen by a doctor," she stressed again. "Even if what you're dealing with is the worst-case scenario—" and by that she meant Alzheimer's, though she couldn't bring herself to say the word out loud "—there are medications that might help slow the disease's progress."

"I know, but if he doesn't want to go, I can't make him." Chase sighed heavily. "He's a grown man, Ella. It's not as if I have medical power of attorney or guardianship and can call the shots for him."

Two things Chase apparently had considered.

"What about Owen? Can you enlist his help?"

"I think Owen is more concerned with staying in the board's good graces than anything else."

"He must realize how serious this is."

"He does, which is why he agrees with those board members who want Elliot removed." Chase shook his head. "Maybe he's right. Maybe they all are. If Elliot continues to decline…"

"All the more reason for you to make your uncle see reason and get to the doctor."

"Haven't you been listening?" Frustration sharpened his tone. "I've tried. In the past week alone, I've consulted some of the best specialists in the country, but Elliot refuses to cooperate and until he does, my hands are tied."

Chase had a point, but Ella was determined. Where there was a will...

"Trick him," she said.

"What?"

"Use his confusion to your advantage. Tell him you're going to lunch or to a movie or for a walk in the park, since he is so fond of those, and then take him to see a specialist. Insist on a full battery of tests once you're there."

"I can't—"

"You can," she said firmly. "For his sake, Chase, you need to stop burying your head in the sand and take action."

The car left the road amid a squeal of tires, fishtailing briefly on the gravel shoulder.

"Let's get something straight!" Chase shouted as soon as they came to a stop. "I'm not burying my head in the sand. I know my uncle is not well. I know he's getting worse. I know, dammit!"

He thumped the steering wheel with his fist for emphasis. Gone was the man who was always in control. In his place sat someone who was frustrated and frightened and at a loss for how to proceed. Someone Ella understood perfectly and could sympathize with, since she'd walked in similar shoes, although hers had sported four-inch heels and a hefty designer price tag.

She placed a hand over one of his fists, accepting his rage, since, ultimately, it wasn't directed at her.

"It's okay to be angry and scared."

"I'm not—"

"You are. Anyone would be."

"He's all I have," Chase said quietly.

"Then you need to get him help."

He turned, eyes bright, gaze searching. She waited, sure he was about to say something important. In the end, he rested his forehead against hers but said nothing at all.

The barbecue was well under way when they arrived at Sandra's parents' home. Ella wasn't sure Chase would stay, despite what he'd said at his uncle's house. She would understand, too. He had a lot on his plate emotionally. He might not be up to attending a party where he likely knew no one and would be forced to make small talk.

But he gave his car keys to the valet without any hesitation. As they walked around to the backyard where the festivities were in full swing, he took Ella's hand. The glance that accompanied his gesture seemed almost like a dare, or a challenge to her earlier claim that they weren't a proper couple. Ella's heart bumped unsteadily, the telltale cadence at odds with what her head kept insisting about the impermanence of their relationship.

She hadn't been looking for a man, much less one she could easily lose her heart to if she weren't careful. She'd been after a job, self-sufficiency, a fresh start. She'd eschewed Madame Maroushka's premonition that she would meet a tall, handsome, fair-haired stranger. Even after she'd encountered Chase and sexual sparks had begun to fly, Ella had considered the romance blooming between them a lovely, if fleeting, bonus. She'd been doing her damnedest not to confuse it with true love and happily ever after.

If there was one thing her mother's premature death and her father's fall from grace had made clear, it was that Ella couldn't rely on others for her happiness. It was up to her to find contentment when and where she could, and she had. Still, she could admit that something had been missing.

Someone.

Chase squeezed her hand and she knew exactly what and who. For all of their differences, they did have a surprising amount in common. The longer she knew him, the more things she discovered they shared. She wasn't sure how she felt about that. Especially since she knew he wasn't looking for a relationship any more than she had been. He was passing through. Other than his uncle's presence here, everything about New York was temporary for Chase, from the penthouse he was subleasing to the office at the Trumbull headquarters.

"Ella! Chase! Over here."

Across the crowded lawn, Sandra, flanked by her boyfriend and her mother, was waving her arms. She would have been impossible to miss anyway. She was wearing a bright orange sundress, the color the perfect complement to her dark hair, making Ella feel a bit boring in the turquoise dress she had on, despite the sparkly silver belt that rode low on her waist. As Ella drew closer, however, it was her friend's footwear that she envied. The wedge espadrilles were a much wiser choice than Ella's high pumps, whose spike heels were already sinking into the grass.

"Hi, Sandra."

"I expected you earlier. Is everything…all right?"

That depended on one's definition, Ella thought wryly. Between Elliot's precarious mental state and her deepening feelings for Chase, spike heels weren't the only reason for Ella's shaky balance. But she told her friend, "Yes. Everything is fine. Sorry. I didn't mean for you to worry. The meeting with Chase's uncle ran a little longer than I expected."

"Well, I'm glad you could make it. *Both* of you," she said meaningfully, before introducing Chase to her mother.

"It's nice to meet you," Mrs. Chesterfield said, taking Chase's hand in both of hers.

"Thank you for having me. Ella tells me that you do this every year to raise funds for diabetes research."

"Yes." The older woman's lips pursed momentarily. "It's a nasty disease. A cure is long overdue."

"Agreed. I forgot my checkbook, but I want to make a personal donation to the cause, one that Trumbull Toys will gladly match."

"Oh, that's wonderful!" Mrs. Chesterfield clapped her hands together. "Thank you."

"That reminds me," Ella said, pulling a check from her purse. When she handed it to Sandra's mother, the older woman gasped at the amount, which admittedly was significant, especially for Ella. "Ella, dear. My goodness! This is very generous. Are you sure?"

"I'm positive. I haven't been able to contribute anything the past couple of years."

Mrs. Chesterfield waved one elegant hand. "You know that doesn't matter to us."

"I know." But it mattered to Ella. She'd vowed to herself that once she'd gotten back into the black financially, she would make up for the lean years. "I'm gainfully employed now."

"Yes, you are." The older woman beamed proudly. "How is the planning for Chase's uncle's party coming, Ella?"

"I'm making headway. I have a lot to learn and not a lot of time to learn it," she admitted before she could think better of it.

She glanced at Chase. He appeared to be taking her confession in stride.

In fact, he said, "Ella may not have much experience, but she is doing an amazing job."

Did she detect a hint of surprise?

"Oh, I have no doubt of that." Sandra's mother smiled fondly and gave Ella's arm a squeeze. "She has always been a very resourceful young woman."

"It helps that I've been to a lot of really great parties over the years, including this one." Ella smiled.

"Next year, you're not only going to be attending this party, Ella, you'll be handling the plans for it," Sandra said. "Isn't that so, Mom?"

"It is. I can't think of anyone I would trust more."

Ella was speechless. Sandra had made the claim before, but this was the first time Ella had heard it from what she considered the voice of authority.

"Mrs. Chesterfield, I don't know what to say."

"Yes, will do."

"Yes! It will be my privilege."

"A privilege for which you will be paid. Oh, and that reminds me. Sandra mentioned that you were looking for a reputable company that rents tents, tables and chairs. I have the number for the one we use every year. We've never had reason to complain. They always set up and break down on time."

"Great! Thanks."

"And I've jotted down some other resources you might want to consider for that job or others. Caterers, disc jockeys, bands and the like. Let's go into the house—"

"Oh, no. Later is fine. Really. I don't want to take you away from your guests."

"It's no trouble. Besides, later I won't remember my name much less where I put my notes," the older woman added on a laugh. She tucked her arm through Ella's. "You don't mind, do you, Chase? I'll bring her right back. I promise."

"Not at all."

"Cole and I will keep him company while you're gone," Sandra said.

As Chase watched Ella walk away, the guilt he'd been keeping at bay rushed in for a vicious attack. She was amazing.

At his uncle's house, her instincts had proved spot-on time
and again. On her own, she'd reached many of the same
conclusions the veteran planner he'd hired behind Ella's
back had shared. And, she'd proved far more creative. Sandra's mother's vote of confidence only made him feel even
worse for doubting Ella.

"You look like you need a drink, Chase," Cole said.

What he needed was to come clean, but when? How?

"I can recommend the daiquiris. They're excellent." Sandra took a sip of the one in her hand. The glass included a
skewer full of fruit and a dainty paper umbrella.

"The beer is ice cold," Cole supplied on a chuckle as he
nodded to his bottle.

"Sounds good."

Sandra rolled her eyes before saying, "I'll be right back."
She got even by handing her fru-fru drink to her boyfriend.
"Hold this and keep Chase company."

While she was gone, another couple stopped to talk to
Cole. The man was tall, athletic, with a smile that belonged
in an advertisement for teeth whitening. The woman was
classically pretty and reed-thin. Her honey-blond hair was
stick straight and pulled back from her oval face by a ribbon headband. She wore canvas sneakers, khaki walking
shorts, a pink sweater set, pearls and an air of superiority.

Her clothing and accessories were prep-school chic, exactly the sort of outfit that complemented her boyfriend's
tame attire. Until recently, Chase had been a fan of the look.
Lately, however, he'd grown fond of animal prints, bright
colors and dangerously high heels.

It wasn't until Cole made the introduction that Chase
realized who they were: Bradley and Bernadette. Ella's
ex and ex-stepsister. God help him. There was no way to
make a graceful escape now. He thought longingly about
the beer Sandra had gone to fetch. What he would give to
have it in hand since he had a bad feeling he would need it

to get through the next several minutes, especially if Ella returned.

It wasn't like Chase to draw comparisons, but he couldn't help doing so. And he didn't like what he concluded. He seemed an awful lot like Bradley. They probably employed the same tailor, visited the same barber. Hell, they probably had the same handicap in golf. Was that why Chase appealed to her? A replacement for the man who'd dumped her? Ella had claimed that she was over Bradley, that it had never been as serious on her side as it had seemed to be on his. That while everyone else had been sure they'd been heading to "I do," she'd never shared their certainty. But… Suddenly, the very casualness with which she approached her relationship with Chase began to chafe.

As for Bernadette, she was nothing like Ella. They were polar opposites in fact, not only in the way they dressed and wore their hair, but how they comported themselves. Ella was vivacious, gregarious, an extravert. Bernadette, meanwhile, whose mere posture oozed self-importance, came across as not only conceited, but decidedly dull.

"This is Chase Trumbull," Cole said, completing the introduction.

Bradley took the name in stride, shaking Chase's hand. Meanwhile, his fiancée's eyes lit up like twin Christmas trees.

"Chase Trumbull," she repeated slowly. "My mother mentioned running in to you not long ago at The Colton. You were having dinner with my stepsister, Ella Sanborn. Mother said you had hired Ella to plan a party. I hope you got your money back."

Droll laughter followed.

"Money's worth, you mean," he said.

"Excuse me?"

"I think you meant to say, you hoped I got my money's

worth. And, yes, I did. Ella did an outstanding job. Several of my guests asked for her card."

Okay, only one and it was Elliot, but the white lie was warranted.

"I'm glad for Ella," Bradley put in. "She's had a rough time of it."

Despite his defense, maybe even because of it, Chase wanted to plow his fist into the guy's face. After all, part of Ella's rough time could be laid at the toes of the man's shiny penny loafers.

"Bradley!" Bernadette gasped.

"Bradley's right. It's not her fault that her father's name got dragged through the mud," Cole added. He had drained his beer during the exchange and was now sipping from Sandra's daiquiri.

"My stepsister is hardly a charity case."

"Ella's no charity case, I agree. But I have to correct you on another matter." And by correct, Chase meant put Bernadette in her place. "Ella is no longer your stepsister."

Bernadette's eyes narrowed but she rallied quickly. "That's right. And, thank God. You know who her father is, right?"

"Oscar Sanborn." Chase nodded. "The man is a legend."

"You mean a pariah. My mother had the good sense to leave him after he was indicted."

"On charges for which he was later cleared."

"Oscar was lucky," she sneered.

"More like innocent."

It came as no surprise that the distinction made little difference to Bernadette. She said, "Either way, he'll never work on Wall Street again. And his reputation is toast. My mother left before he could ruin hers."

"For better or worse, richer or poorer. Vows can be so damned inconvenient," Chase said dryly.

Cole started coughing, although his smile made it clear

he was really camouflaging a laugh. Bernadette wasn't fooled. She looked as if she could have cheerfully gouged out his eyes before moving on to Chase's.

"Ella is a pariah, too."

"Which was why old Brad here pulled a disappearing act, too," Chase retorted.

"Hey—" the other man said only to be cut off by his fiancée.

"He traded up. Poor Ella," Bernadette purred with far more glee than sympathy in her tone. "She can't get invited to the A-list parties so now she is trying the backdoor approach. Reinventing herself as a party planner is creative, I will give her that, but please. She's no party planner."

"She's doing a credible imitation," Chase shot back. And she was, which made his duplicity all the more unpalatable.

Cole, trying to salvage the situation or at least keep it from deteriorating any further, tried to change the subject.

"How do you feel about horses, Chase? I own a couple of thoroughbreds, including a yearling that shows real promise on the track."

"Bradley is looking to purchase a foal sired by Peerpoint's Return. He placed in the Preakness last year and finished fourth in the Derby the year before that," Bernadette inserted importantly. "With the right trainer, Bradley thinks Peerpoint's Return could have done better."

"Really?" Chase replied. He was supposed to be impressed. That was what she expected. He'd been around enough people like Bernadette to understand that. Hell, he'd dated enough women like her. Women who liked to drop names and who used others to elevate their social stature.

More than ever, Chase appreciated Ella's authenticity and her sense of humor, which she was willing to direct at herself on occasion.

"Can I give you some advice?" he said to Bradley.

"Advice?"

Chase shook his head. "No, I guess it's really more like an observation." He leaned in close to be sure he had the other man's full attention. It was merely a bonus that Bernadette leaned in, as well. "You bet on the wrong horse."

"What?" Bradley said at the same time Bernadette sputtered incredulously, "I…I… You can't speak to me that way. Bradley, you're not going to let him speak to me that way, are you?"

Chase answered for him. "You should have paid attention, Bernadette. Did he speak up on Ella's behalf when people started saying hurtful things?"

"That's not the same."

"Horse of a different color?" Chase shook his head. "But you both deserve each other. Excuse me."

He spied Ella through the crowd. She was a welcome sight. He wasn't entirely comfortable with the feelings she inspired in him, but he couldn't deny them. The only thing tempering his reaction was guilt. He gave in to the overwhelming urge to kiss her.

"Wow," she murmured as he drew back. Out of deference for their surroundings, he'd kept the kiss short. "What was that for?"

"Do I need a reason?" he asked.

"No." She wrapped her arms around his shoulders and pulled him back for another quick lip-lock. Afterward she murmured, "Neither do I."

"You're special, Ella."

He'd intended the words as a compliment, but she frowned.

"Uh-oh, something really is wrong. Are you…dumping me?"

"What? No! Why would you say that?"

"Whenever someone calls you special, especially someone you're dating. Not that we're really a couple—"

"We're a couple," he said.

"Oh."

"And I'm not dumping you."

"Oh."

Chase framed her face with his hands. "And you are special, Ella. Special, amazing, gorgeous, funny—"

Her lips curved. "Don't forget smart."

"I was getting to that." He smiled, too, before pulling her close.

"I didn't hear a sexy in there," she murmured against his cheek.

"That's a given."

"You're special, too," she whispered. Her breath tickled his ear when she added, "I'll show you exactly how special later tonight."

He didn't point out that she would be staying over at Sandra's parents' house. It was her words, the promise behind them, that touched him in a way no mere sexual fantasy could.

Sandra came up then with his beer.

"I understand from Cole that I missed quite an exchange while I was off getting this," she said with a grin as she handed Chase the bottle.

"I'm really sorry about that. I should have kept my big mouth shut." To Ella he said, "I just had the displeasure of meeting Bradley and Bernadette."

"Oh, God!" She glanced around. "I was really hoping that with as many people as are here, we wouldn't run into them."

"No such luck, I'm afraid."

She wrinkled her nose. "Was it bad?"

"That depends on who you ask," Sandra supplied. She rose up on tiptoe and kissed Chase's cheek. "That's for being a white knight."

"Ella hardly qualifies as a damsel in distress," Chase argued.

He meant it, too. He'd never met a woman more capable

of taking care of herself, even if her methods were unconventional. But being capable didn't mean she couldn't also be vulnerable. She could be used, hurt. She had been. Just as she had been underestimated by a lot of people, present company included. Chase's biggest worry was that he would hurt her, too.

"Am I missing something?" Ella wanted to know.

Sandra ignored the question. "You're right, Chase. Our Ella can save herself. She's proved as much more than once during the past few years. Still, it's nice to know someone has her back for a change. So thanks."

Not sure how to reply, Chase sipped his beer.

"White knight, hmm?" Ella said.

He shrugged, uncomfortable with the title. "I gave it my best shot."

To Sandra, Ella said, "We can't stay long."

Both of them gaped at her.

"But you were going to spend the night," Sandra reminded her.

"I know. Change of plans." Ella winked. "I promised Chase I was going to show him something."

Sandra's expression morphed from confused to knowing. "I bet you did."

By the time they'd reached the city, the rain that was predicted for the evening had started to fall.

Chase circled the block three times without finding a place for his car. When he reached the front of her building a fourth time, he double-parked in front of the entrance.

"You can't park here," Ella told him.

"I just did."

"But you *can't*. You'll get ticketed or, worse, your car will be towed."

Neither of her dire predictions appeared to have any effect on Chase's decision. For a man who generally colored inside the lines, he suddenly seemed willing to break form. He got out of the car, came around to her side with an umbrella. White knight, Sandra had called him. Ella agreed, and not only because of this gallant gesture. She might not need saving, but that didn't mean she couldn't appreciate a man who would go to bat for her.

Huddled together under the umbrella, they hurried to the door. Under the awning, she turned.

"Go back and move your car."

"I don't give a damn about the car."

"A man who doesn't give a damn about his car? Be still my heart," she teased. Then, "Really, Chase, you should move it."

"After," he said. "You promised to show me something."

He took the keys from her hand, unlocked the door and followed her inside.

"I wish I lived on the first floor," she muttered as they started up.

"I don't know. I have a new appreciation for stairs."

"You...what?" She glanced over her shoulder and understanding dawned. His gaze was on her butt.

"This must be how you stay so toned."

"It's an excellent cardio workout," she agreed. "Especially if you take the steps at a jog, and it's a lot cheaper than a gym membership."

It was her turn to take in his physique. Despite the umbrella's semi-protection, his white shirt was plastered to the contours of an impressive chest and rock-solid abs. She couldn't wait to peel it off him.

Suddenly energized, she took off.

"Hey!" he shouted. "What are you doing?"

Ella's husky laughter rang out, echoing down the stairwell, before she called over her shoulder, "Seeing if you can keep up!"

Halfway up the first flight, she glanced back. She hadn't

heard any footsteps behind her. She figured Chase had decided she was crazy. But he was grinning—*grinning!*—and looking hot despite his soggy clothes.

"What are you waiting for?" she asked.

"Just giving you a head start." He nodded to her feet. "It's only fair given those heels."

"I don't expect special treatment, but I'll take it." Feeling equal parts ridiculous and turned on, she continued up.

This time, Chase followed fast on her heels. She could hear him coming, the leather soles of his shoes slapping the risers with rhythmic force. The sound was exhilarating and she hoped indicative of what was to come.

Laughter bubbled out when she reached the third landing. Before she could start up the final flight, however, Chase stole her breath by wrapping his hands around her waist and hauling her backward. His body was hard against hers. Steamy from the combination of heated skin and sodden clothes. His fingers found the hem of her dress and began working it up her thighs. A moan escaped when he reached the band of her panties.

"My apartment—"

"Too far," he groaned.

He had a point.

Ella had never had sex in a stairwell, though she'd fantasized in great detail about doing the deed in an elevator. But that wasn't what gave her heart a start. Chase, Mr. Conservative, was flouting convention in ways she hadn't dreamed him capable.

"You're full of surprises," she told him.

"Just wait."

And with that he proceeded to prove his point.

CHAPTER TWELVE

CHASE WOKE UP smiling the following morning and not only because of the naked woman whose leg was tossed over both of his.

He replayed the events of the previous evening. Sex in a stairwell? That wasn't like him. Neither were the scenes in his dining room and office, but damned if he could find fault with the outcome.

He glanced around for a clock, but couldn't find one, which came as no real surprise. Ella was the sort of person who ran on her own time. That should annoy him, would have if she didn't get things done when they needed to be done. And look sexy doing it. He found himself smiling again.

Ella moved, and her thigh slid up his legs. Chase's grin gave way to a groan. Would he ever get enough of her? Did he want to?

"Good morning," she murmured, pushing hair out of her eyes. On a throaty chuckle she added, "Someone's wide awake."

"I was just thinking about last night," he replied.

"Yeah? What a coincidence. She pushed to a kneeling position on the lumpy futon mattress. The pose, along with her tumbled hair and sleepy eyes, were the stuff of fantasies. And that was before she straddled him. "So was I."

* * *

Chase cursed and crumpled up the page he'd been reading in *The Wall Street Journal*. Damn, Kellerman! Once again, Trumbull Toys' top competitor had beaten them to market with a remarkably similar toy—this time a life-size talking doll.

Kellerman's CEO was quoted in the article predicting the doll would be one of the most sought-after toys for girls between the ages of three and nine that Christmas. Even though it was summer, marketing had already geared up for the holiday shopping season.

Chase was in a foul mood and spoiling for a fight when he heard his cousin step into the reception area from the elevator. Owen was whistling, as if he had not a care in the world.

Chase grabbed the paper and got up.

Owen was at the basketball hoop that Chase had had re-installed. The reception area also had been repainted from nondescript beige to a vibrant red...the same shade Chase was seeing at the moment.

"Can I have a word with you in private?" he asked Owen.

Owen dribbled the ball twice before taking his shot. It hit the rim and bounced off. Chase captured the rebound. "Now."

"I guess it was too much to hope that the changes you made around here meant you were no longer such a stick in the mud."

Chase let the comment slide. He had more important issues to discuss.

"Have you seen this?" he said as soon as they were in Chase's office. He tossed the wadded up newspaper at his cousin.

"More bad news, I take it," Owen replied, throwing it in the trash can without a second glance.

"How did you guess? Or maybe you don't need to guess. Maybe you know exactly what the article says."

"What in the hell is that supposed to mean?" Gone was Owen's easygoing smile. He was pissed. That made two of them.

"Like you don't know," Chase snarled.

"If you're going to accuse me of something, be a man and come right out and say it."

Fine, Chase thought. He moved forward until he and his cousin stood nose-to-nose. "I think you're the one who gave or sold our information to Kellerman."

"You think I'm the leak?"

To Chase's surprise, Owen didn't appear defensive as much as…hurt? He had to be wrong.

"Tell me you're not."

"And you'll believe me? Right?" Owen snorted. "I could swear on my mother's grave and it wouldn't change your mind."

"I want to trust you, but let's face it. You haven't given me many reasons to over the years."

"Saint Chase." Owen poked him in the chest. "The up-standing Trumbull to whom I've always come a distant second."

"Your jealousy has gotten old. For God's sake, Owen, the past is the past. We're adults now. Act like one. This company needs you. Elliot needs you."

"Don't talk to me about my father and what he needs. While you were in California a lot of things changed." Owen's rage boiled up and over. "And then you came back, riding to the rescue when the bottom fell out. Saint Chase. But even you can't make this right. In fact, the more you try to keep my father on, the worse off this company will be."

"What in the hell are you talking about?"

"I'm pretty sure I know who the leak is."

Shocked that his cousin was not only admitting that he

now believed there was a leak, but that he knew the person's identity, Chase demanded, "Why haven't you said anything?"

"Because…it doesn't matter."

"How can you say that? Whoever it is needs to be fired. Hell, they need to be prosecuted. They've cost this company hundreds of thousands of dollars, perhaps even millions."

Owen met his gaze.

"The leak is my dad, Chase. He's the one who has been giving Kellerman the inside scoop on the hot products coming down the pipeline."

"No! You're wrong."

"I'm not. I wish I were, but…" Owen shook his head. "I had Kellerman followed after the T. rex fiasco. Did you know that he goes for regular walks in the park?"

"What?"

"When I questioned Dad about it, it was clear he sometimes forgot that he and Roy are competitors rather than friends or partners. My guess was that Dad was innocently sharing information with Roy."

"And Roy wouldn't be above using it given their history."

"Or mentioning to people in the industry that Elliot was going senile."

Chase swore softly. It added up. "Why didn't you tell me, Owen? You knew I suspected a leak."

"First, I didn't have irrefutable proof that Dad was sharing information." His cousin bristled then. "Besides, he's my father. I'm capable of dealing with him without either your help or your interference."

"By buying him a treadmill in an attempt to keep him from going for walks and then siding with the board to oust him?"

Owen snarled, "And what would you have done? You refused to face the fact that Dad's memory had become an issue. He's no longer capable of running the company.

Hell, without Dermott, he might not be capable of living independently much longer. Don't you think it kills me to see him like this? Now that Mom is gone, he's all I have."

Chase had said something similar to Ella. Apparently, both he and Owen had forgotten that they also had each other. Now was not the time to figure out if they could salvage their old relationship or forge a new one now that they were adults. But they did have to put aside their differences, past and present, to do what was best for the man who raised them both.

"If we were to get him some help…" Chase couldn't go on. When he glanced at Owen, his cousin's eyes were bright, too.

"Maybe. But right now, he needs to step down so that we can save his legacy."

"From the beginning, he's seen the wake as his swan song," Chase said slowly. Sometimes it had seemed as if Chase were fighting harder to save Elliot's position than Elliot was. Maybe, despite his declining mental state, part of his uncle had known it was time to step down.

"It might be a good time to make an official announcement," Owen said. "Especially since the full board will be there and so will the media."

Chase nodded. "I'll mention it to Ella. She's planning a retrospective of Elliot's career. It would make sense to do it right before that."

For the first time in a long time, the cousins were in agreement.

Chase looked like hell. That was Ella's first thought when she got off the elevator. He stood in the penthouse's foyer, his complexion ashen, his features pinched. He'd called three hours earlier from the clinic where he and Owen had taken Elliot to be evaluated by a team of specialists including neurologists and endocrinologists. They hadn't given

Elliot a chance to refuse. They'd used his confusion to their advantage, as Ella had suggested. It was for the best, although looking at Chase right now, she wished it hadn't been necessary. The man was gutted.

She didn't wait for him to speak. Instead, she rushed forward and wrapped her arms around his neck, pulling him to her to offer the only comfort she could.

"Hard day?" she asked after a moment.

"And a long one."

Arm in arm, they walked into the living room, where they settled on the couch. "What's the diagnosis?"

"They don't have all the test results back yet. A vitamin deficiency has been ruled out. As has stress and grief over my aunt's death, although both likely exacerbated any underlying condition."

"What about Alzheimer's?" She held her breath.

"It's still in the running, but they're also checking to see if a metabolic disorder could be the culprit."

He named off a couple different kinds of conditions that might be the cause.

"If it is, would it be reversible?"

"Maybe, but not necessarily. It would depend on the amount of brain damage that has occurred." He swore before saying again, "Brain damage. God! If I'd gotten him to the doctor sooner—"

"Don't! Don't do that to yourself."

They sat in silence for several minutes, holding hands. Then Ella asked, "What happens at the company now?"

Gaze fixed on the ceiling, Chase said, "The board already had plans to vote on Elliot's removal as CEO. I'm pretty sure they had the votes to do it. Owen and I have informed the members of Elliot's plans to step down on his own."

"He's still okay with that?" she asked.

"He is, especially since he gets to do it at the wake on his own terms."

"Going out with a bang," she murmured.

"Yeah. I have little doubt the stock will rebound several points once the official announcement is made."

That was good news, but the current situation made it impossible to celebrate.

"Will you take over Elliot's position?"

It was what his uncle wanted, she knew, even if ultimately it wasn't Elliot's call. But Chase shook his head. "Owen will. You know, I think he'll do a good job."

For the past few weeks, the cousins had been working in concert. A truce had been called. A new bond, albeit a fragile one, was being forged. Ella was glad the cousins were no longer feuding, just as she was glad that the company's fortunes would soon start improving, but she couldn't help but be worried about what the future held for her and Chase.

With the leak plugged and a new executive at the helm in New York, surely it would be only a matter of time before Chase returned to his job heading up Trumbull's offices on the West Coast.

For one wild moment, she considered returning with him. She could plan parties anywhere. But reality intruded. Ella's father was here, and Oscar needed her. Besides, Chase hadn't asked her to go. While she had succeeded in tumbling head over high heels in love with him, and she knew he liked her—a lot—he hadn't used the big L-word to describe his feelings, nor had he hinted at a future together.

C for casual, she reminded herself.

In this instance, *C* did not stand for commitment.

With one week to go before Elliot's party, Ella was spending most of her waking hours putting out fires, from revising the number of confirmed attendees thanks to late-arriving

RSVPs, to meeting with the company hired to construct the custom platform to go over the inground pool. The one delivered was the wrong size—too narrow by three feet.

If not for massive quantities of caffeine, she wouldn't have the energy to get out of bed in the mornings, especially after the nights she spent with Chase.

The man was inventive, she thought with a sly smile as she recalled their bedroom adventures from the previous evening.

Afterward, since she had a meeting not far from there in the morning, she'd stayed over at his penthouse. She was alone in it now. Chase had already left for his office. Ella finished up the cup of coffee he'd so thoughtfully brewed for her, and was on her way to the elevator when his phone rang. Figuring it was him, she answered without glancing at the caller ID. But it wasn't Chase. It was a woman.

"Hi. This is Danica Fleming. May I speak to Chase Trumbull, please?"

Danica Fleming? Why did that name ring a bell?

"I'm sorry," Ella replied. "You just missed him. May I take a message?"

Okay, so Ella made the offer not only to be polite, but because her curiosity was begging to be satisfied.

"That's all right," the woman replied. "I was just wondering how things are working out for his uncle's party."

Far from being satisfied, Ella's curiosity was now good and piqued.

"Who did you say you were again?" she asked.

"Danica Fleming from Fleming Event Planning Services."

No wonder the name had seemed familiar. The outfit was one of the largest and best known planning services in Manhattan. And Chase had been in touch with its owner about his uncle's Irish wake?

"From what I know, everything is working out fine," Ella told her.

"That's terrific. I hope the suggestions I passed along helped." Danica chuckled before confiding, "He was pretty concerned that the inexperienced young woman his uncle insisted on using was in way over her head."

"She's pretty green," Ella managed around the lump in her throat.

And clueless, she thought. All of the praise he'd heaped on her efforts in recent weeks along with his encouragement now rang insincere. And those *suggestions,* some of which Ella had implemented, they'd come from a veteran planner. A planner for whose expertise he surely was paying.

Ella could understand why Chase had done it. She had been in well over her head at the beginning. Hell, maybe she still was, although she'd begun to think that she had clawed her way to the surface through sheer determination and had been treading water quite well for a newbie.

His lack of faith wouldn't have hurt so much if they weren't involved. If she hadn't fallen in love with him.

But they were involved. She had fallen in love. And she'd hoped, apparently foolishly, that he might be falling in love with her, too. But how could Chase love her and fail to be honest with her about this?

He'd gone behind her back. Even now, with Elliot set to announce his retirement, Trumbull's stock getting ready to rebound and the wake no longer in danger of becoming the PR fiasco, Chase still hadn't been truthful.

Even worse than deceiving her, he didn't believe in her.

After hanging up, Ella felt sick. But she had an appointment with the caterer and scores of other details to see to between now and that evening. Because she wanted to sit down on Chase's couch—the very couch on which they had cuddled together to watch a movie the previous night—and have a good cry, she straightened her spine, grabbed her purse and punched the button for the elevator.

She would be damned if she would fall apart now.

"This is a nice surprise," Chase said when Ella tapped at his office door later that afternoon.

He probably wasn't going to think so after he heard what she had to say, but she worked up a smile. "Got a minute?"

"That's about all. Owen and I have a conference call scheduled with the new head of the California office."

That took the wind out of her sails. "The new head of the—"

"California office." Chase grinned. "I've decided to stay in New York."

Her traitorous heart thumped with joy. If not for the call she'd intercepted, she might have made a fool out of herself and assumed that his feelings for her played a role in his decision. She knew better.

"That's nice. I'm happy for you," she replied, keeping her tone neutral. "Your family's here."

"More than that is here," he replied.

"Well, sure. The company's headquarters."

Chase frowned. "Ella? Is everything okay?"

"Why do you ask?"

"I guess I thought the news would be greeted with a little more enthusiasm than that."

"I'm all out of enthusiasm," she shot back.

He nodded, as if he understood. "You're under a lot of stress right now. Let me guess. More RSVPs have trickled in since you gave the final count to the caterer this morning. Did you round up the number by a couple dozen like I suggested?" he asked.

Ella gritted her teeth. "Did you suggest that?"

"Yes. Just this morning." He sounded confused with a side helping of wary thrown in.

"Oh. I thought maybe the suggestion had come from Danica."

Ella watched the color drain from his face. If he denied it now, she'd…she'd… Okay, she wasn't sure what she would do, but it wasn't going to be pleasant for either of them.

Chase didn't deny it. He nodded and said, "Danica Fleming."

"That's right. The owner of the highly respected Fleming Event Planning Services."

"Ella, I can ex—"

She cut him off. He could explain in a minute. First, she needed to recite the pithy monologue she'd worked out on the cab ride over.

"She called your home this morning. I picked up, thinking it might be you. Imagine my surprise when, after Danica identified herself, she asked how the—and I quote—inexperienced party planner your uncle had insisted on hiring was making out. Oh, and she wanted to know if the suggestions she'd given you to give me had helped."

"Ella—"

"When did you hire her, Chase?"

"It doesn't matter when. What matters is that you've proved yourself more than capable of handling the event."

"Proved?" She recoiled as if slapped. "I didn't realize I had to prove anything to you."

To herself, sure. And to Elliot since he was her client. But to Chase? To the man she loved?

"That came out wrong," he said, rising and coming around his desk. But she stepped away when he reached for her. "What I meant is, for a woman who had never planned a party before putting together dinner for eight in my penthouse a little over a month ago, you've done an outstanding job. I've been amazed by your attention to detail and intuitive sense of what's needed to be done. The way you've handled vendors and the bargains you've struck. You're a natural."

"A natural," she scoffed. "Right. You consider me such a *natural* that you've had a seasoned professional waiting in the wings in case I screwed up."

"It's not like that," he began.

"It's *exactly* like that, Chase. For all of your talk, you haven't thought I could do this." God, that hurt. Ella's chest ached and tears threatened. She refused to shed them. Not here. Not now. Not in front of the man she loved. A man who apparently had as little faith in her as Bernadette and Camilla and the other people from Ella's past.

"I haven't spoken to Danica for weeks, Ella."

Another time, his words might have made her feel better. Right now, raw from this discovery, she could only tell him, "You haven't spoken to her in weeks, yet in all that time, you never once mentioned her to me."

"It wasn't like that."

"You didn't trust me." He reached for her, but Ella backed away. "You didn't have faith in me. Bernadette and Camilla, even my own father expressed doubts or outright disbelief that I could do this. But you…"

She shook her head, unable to go on.

"I know it seems like that, but when I called Danica, I didn't know you, Ella."

She didn't point out that they had to have been sleeping together. They'd gone to Chase's apartment immediately after Elliot had refused to let her quit.

"Okay." She nodded. "You didn't know me then. The point I am making is that you've *known* me pretty well for several weeks now. You didn't level with me, Chase. Were you ever going to?"

He shoved a hand through his hair, drawing her attention to the cowlick. She loved that cowlick, but maybe it was a sign of bad luck.

"Honestly, with everything else that has been going on, I just forgot."

That was his explanation? He forgot? Ella's chest ached along with her throat. It was just as well that the door opened and Owen entered.

"Oh? Sorry. I didn't realize you were busy."

"That's all right," Ella told him. With one last look at Chase, she added, "We're finished."

CHAPTER THIRTEEN

THE EARLY MORNING sunshine coming through the bedroom blinds should have put Chase in a good mood. Today was his uncle's big party and bad weather would have been a disaster. But it was difficult to be in a good mood when he hadn't spoken to Ella in nearly a week.

She hadn't only walked out of his office on Monday. She'd walked out of his life.

We're finished.

Two words that had struck his heart like an arrow finding the bull's-eye. Still, he hadn't thought she'd meant them.

But since then she'd refused all of his calls. She hadn't replied to his text messages or emails. And when he'd stopped by her apartment, knowing full well that she was home, she'd ignored the buzzer. Chase had almost wished the damned brick had been back, propping open the main entrance. At least that way he would be able to get inside, with only a single door between them, rather than two doors and four flights of stairs. Perhaps if he were that much closer he might have been able to get her to listen.

He had plenty to say, too. He would start with a heart-felt apology and grovel if need be. He was that desperate to make her understand. She had to believe him when he said that his concerns with her abilities as a party planner had evaporated over time, and then everything happening with his uncle had become his focus. He believed in Ella. It was impossible not to. He'd never met another person so determined.

Then he had another admission to make. One that had taken him a while to wrap his mind around. One that still filled him with equal amounts of awe and nerves. He could only hope she was ready to hear it. And that she felt the same way.

It was just after ten o'clock when Chase arrived at his uncle's estate. The driveway was jammed with an assortment of delivery trucks, and both the house and the grounds were a hive of activity. Chase found his uncle in the study, playing cards with Dermott. Elliot was happy, if a bit befuddled at times. His condition had stabilized now that they'd diagnosed his condition as vascular dementia brought on by high blood pressure, but the doctors were clear that some of the damage to his brain was permanent.

While he couldn't run Trumbull Toys, Elliott remained the heart of the company and the de facto head of the creative team. His office was just as he left it, the nameplate on the door more apt than ever. The Purveyor of All Things Fun glanced up at Chase now.

"We can deal you in the next hand, if you'd like," he offered.

"That's all right. I'm looking for Ella."

"The last time I saw her, she was by the pool house," Dermott said.

"Thanks."

Chase turned on his heel, ready to leave. Elliot's words stopped him.

"She's a lovely girl, with a lot on her mind right now. Don't upset her."

"I… What do you mean?"

"The two of you have had a fight."

"She told you?" Chase asked, surprised.

"She didn't need to. I may be a bit loopy at times, but I could figure it out. She's been walking around here like she's planning somebody's funeral for real." Elliot picked up a card from the deck and glanced at it before transferring his gaze to Chase. "Can I give you some advice, my boy?"

"Sure."

"Wait until tonight to seek her out. She has so much to do right now. I've asked a lot of her, planning my wake."

"She's done a great job."

"She has." He beamed. "I knew she had it in her. I could tell the moment I met her. Reminded me of myself when I started out."

His uncle's blind faith made Chase feel doubly disloyal for his doubts.

Elliot was saying, "Once most of the guests are gone and those who are still here are good and sloshed, bring her a glass of something cold along with one for yourself. Toast her success as the fireworks go off."

"Fireworks?" This was the first Chase had heard of them. How had she had managed to pull a permit and line up a pyrotechnics show in a matter of days?

But Elliot was grinning. "I trust you to supply those. You're going to tell her you love her, right?"

Chase was, but first, even though it was going to kill him, he also was going to take his uncle's advice and wait.

Ella had seen Chase arrive. She'd spied his car as it had snaked up the crowded driveway. She'd been too busy to talk to him then, and so she'd been grateful that he hadn't sought her out.

Once guests began arriving, she saw him with Owen and Elliot stationed at the entrance to greet everyone. He was dressed formally, as were his uncle and cousin. He looked gorgeous, perfect. Was it bad of her that she hoped he felt as miserable as she did?

He glanced up once, caught her eye. Then the crowds moved and so did she, losing herself to the throng and to her job. It wasn't only for Elliot's sake that she wanted this party to go off without a glitch. She had a lot to prove.

Dinner went mostly according to plan. She credited the workers overseeing each station for that. They kept the guests moving, the chafing dishes replenished. The Italian station ran out of meatballs early after an entire pan got dropped in the grass. Accidents were to be expected. She overheard a couple of women complaining that the alfredo sauce was too rich, but she chalked that up to taste. With a crowd this size, it was impossible to please everyone. Besides, if they didn't like the alfredo sauce, there were plenty of other dishes to try.

Once dinner was over and the guests were swarming the dessert stations like bees to a hive, Ella spied Chase making his way toward her. Security chose that moment to call her cell about a scuffle between two tabloid reporters.

By the time she'd gotten that and another small crisis settled, she heard the music start. The dancing got under way.

"Are you going to save a dance for me?"

She knew a moment of disappointment when she turned to find Owen. With a polite smiled, she told him, "Sorry. I'm on the clock."

He snapped his fingers. "Damn." Before she could walk away, he added, "Do both yourself and Chase a favor. Don't turn him down if he asks."

"I don't know what you mean."

"I think you do. I don't know what happened between you two. I don't need to know. But this much is clear. My cousin is lost without you. Not all that long ago, I would have been happy about that. Now..." He shrugged. "Give him a second chance, okay?" Owen's tone was filled with irony when he added, "Everyone deserves one."

Ella's heart thumped unsteadily as she watched Owen

walk away. Was she being a hypocrite? She was all for chances—giving people a chance to prove themselves as well as to redeem themselves. Shouldn't she extend the same courtesy to Chase?

As she mulled that, the retrospective of Elliot's career began on the big screen. Ella stayed in the back, out of the way of guests, but she was close enough to hear some of the delighted responses. Elliot was beloved by many and admired by his peers. It only could do his health good to know that, she thought, wiping her damp cheeks.

"I hope those are happy tears," Chase said, coming up alongside her. He held a flute of champagne in each hand. "You did an outstanding job here tonight, Ella."

"Thank you. Of course, the night's not over." She cast a meaningful glance at the champagne. "I'll pass on that. I need to keep a clear head."

"I figured that's what you'd say, which is why it's sparkling cider."

"Oh. Well, in that case."

She took the glass and sipped. Bubbles tickled her nose. Even without the kick of alcohol she started to feel warm. Chase's unwavering gaze didn't help. She'd seen Chase's face reflect anger, interest, frustration, regret, satisfaction and a number of other emotions. She'd never seen this look.

He was humbled, she realized. Contrite. Lost…as his cousin had claimed.

And something more. Something that required not only trust, but forgiveness to survive.

"Can I offer a toast?" he asked.

Chase, Owen and a few other speakers, all of whom had been tapped in advance, had given toasts earlier in Elliot's honor. All of them had been moving and heartfelt. Ella and a lot of other people had wiped away tears afterward.

"Only if you promise not to make me cry again," she

said. "The toast you made for your uncle was very touching."

"Thank you, this one is to Madame Maroushka."

"You're toasting the fortune-teller?" she asked.

"If not for her, we might never have met. I owe her." Chase's voice lost its teasing quality when he went on. "And I owe you an apology, Ella. One I hope you will find it in your heart to accept. I screwed up. I should have mentioned that I'd called Danica Fleming from the beginning, or at the very least when things between us started to get serious."

"How serious are they?" she asked softly.

"I've never felt this way about anyone before, Ella." Chase took her glass and set it, along with his, on a nearby table.

"What are you doing? I thought we were going to toast?"

"I need to be touching you when I bare my soul."

When he put it like that, it was impossible to argue.

"The past several days without you, have been…they've…" When he groped for the right word, she supplied, "Sucked." Chase laughed. "Yeah. They sucked."

"For me, too," She admitted.

He sobered. In fact, she didn't think she'd ever seen Chase quite so serious or intense, when he said, "I hurt you. I didn't mean to, but I did. And for that, I feel awful. I do believe in you, Ella. Maybe I had doubts at first, but—"

"Chase."

He shook his head. "No. I need to say this. If you'll give me another chance, I think I can make you as happy as you've made me. I love you, Ella. I—"

She put her fingers over his lips to stop him from talking. When had the man become so chatty? She needed to get in a few words herself.

Starting with the most important, "I love you, too."

And because it already felt as if an eternity had passed since they'd last kissed, Ella grabbed Chase by the lapels and hauled him close. Just before their mouths met, it occurred to her that Madame Maroushka's supposed vision of Ella and a tall, handsome man at a party had come true.

* * * * *

A sneaky peek at next month...

MODERN
tempted ™

**FRESH, CONTEMPORARY ROMANCES TO TEMPT
ALL LOVERS OF GREAT STORIES**

My wish list for next month's titles...

In stores from 17th January 2014:

☐ No Time Like Mardi Gras — Kimberly Lang

☐ The Last Guy She Should Call — Joss Wood

In stores from 7th February 2014:

☐ Romance For Cynics — Nicola Marsh

☐ Trouble On Her Doorstep — Nina Harrington

Available at WHSmith, Tesco, Asda, Eason, Amazon and Apple

Just can't wait?

0114/31

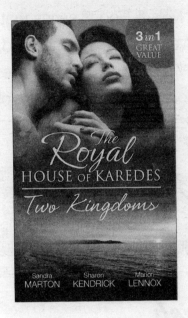

Discover more romance at

www.millsandboon.co.uk

- ❤ WIN great prizes in our exclusive competitions

- ❤ BUY new titles before they hit the shops

- ❤ BROWSE new books and REVIEW your favourites

- ❤ SAVE on new books with the Mills & Boon® Bookclub™

- ❤ DISCOVER new authors

PLUS, to chat about your favourite reads, get the latest news and find special offers:

- Find us on facebook.com/millsandboon
- Follow us on twitter.com/millsandboonuk
- ❤ Sign up to our newsletter at millsandboon.co.uk